Mary Todd Lincoln

Girl of the Bluegrass

Illustrated by Leslie Goldstein

Mary Todd
Lincoln

Girl of the Bluegrass

By Katharine E. Wilkie

Aladdin Paperbacks

Aladdin Paperbacks
An imprint of Simon & Schuster
Children's Publishing Division
1230 Avenue of the Americas
New York, NY 10020
Copyright © 1954, 1960 by the Bobbs-Merrill Company, Inc.
All rights reserved including the right of reproduction
in whole or in part in any form.
First Aladdin Paperbacks edition, 1992

Printed and bound in the United States of America
10   9   8   7   6

Library of Congress Cataloging-in-Publication Data
Wilkie, Katharine Elliott, date.
    Mary Todd Lincoln, girl of the Bluegrass / by Katharine E. Wilkie;
  [illustrated by Leslie Goldstein]. — 1st Aladdin Books ed.
      p.   cm. — (Childhood of Famous Americans)
    Summary: A biography concentrating on the childhood of the
  Kentucky girl who grew up to marry Abraham Lincoln.
    ISBN 0-689-71655-9
    1. Lincoln, Mary Todd, 1818–1882—Juvenile literature.   2. Lincoln,
  Abraham, 1809–1865—Juvenile literature.   3. Presidents—United
  States—Wives—Biography—Juvenile literature.   [1. Lincoln, Mary
  Todd, 1818–1882—Childhood and youth.   2. First ladies.]   I. Goldstein,
  Leslie, ill.   II. Title.   III. Series: Childhood of Famous Americans
  series.
  E457.25.W6   1992
  973.7'092—dc20
  [B]   92-9782

To Bettie, Bunkie and Buddy

Illustrations

Full pages

	PAGE
"Well, there she is."	27
They heard the family coming.	74
It seemed an enchanted scene.	116
"What did you think?"	128
Mary was in her glory.	137
The fairy tale came to life.	163
Mary told her family good-by.	172
Abraham was elected President.	191

Numerous smaller illustrations

Contents

	PAGE
Runaways	11
A New Adventure	20
A New Friend	29
"That Old Blabbing Brook"	38
The Little Railroad	50
Hoop Skirts	64
Surprise from New Orleans	79
An Indian Scare	88

	PAGE
The Journey to Frankfort	100
Invitation to a Ball	112
Mary's Not a Bluestocking	121
A Wedding in the Family	131
The Taming of a Wildcat	141
The Glass Slipper	151
A Trip to Springfield	167
Mrs. Abraham Lincoln	176

★ # Mary Todd Lincoln

Girl of the Bluegrass

Runaways

"I won't be a little lady!" Six-year-old Mary Todd stamped her foot. Her nurse, Mammy Sally, put her hands on her hips. She glared down at the child. Mary scowled up at her.

"Come and get dressed like a good little girl," Mammy Sally pleaded. "You must take off those dirty clothes and put on your white muslin. The ladies will soon be here to have tea with your Aunt Ann Maria."

Mary stamped her foot again. "Let Elizabeth or Frances dress up for them. Or Levi. I guess Ann Maria and George are too little. I certainly don't want to."

She ran from the room. Mammy Sally heard her scampering down the back stairs. A few minutes later there was the clatter of hoofs on the driveway. Mammy Sally rolled her eyes in despair.

"Mary is her daddy's own daughter," she fussed. "Neither of them will listen to a *no* from anybody. Now she has ridden away on that pony. Goodness only knows when she'll be back!"

Meanwhile Mary was cantering down the main street of Lexington, Kentucky, on Snowball. She and the white pony made a pleasing picture. All signs of her ill temper were gone. She rode sidesaddle with grace and ease. Her copper-colored curls might need combing, but they looked pretty in the summer breeze. Her face might need washing, but her blue eyes and happy smile made more than one person on the sidewalk turn to look at her.

It was October, 1825. As Mary rode along, she met several carriages rolling slowly down the street. She waved to the ladies in them. The daughter of Robert S. Todd knew nearly everybody in town. She blew a kiss to the little Frenchman, Monsieur Giron, who was standing at the corner of Main and Mill streets.

Every boy and girl in Lexington knew Monsieur Giron. He owned a confectionery where his Swiss cook made fine cookies and candies. They looked and tasted as though they had been made by magic.

Now Mary and Snowball were passing the courthouse. Another block and they would reach the Phoenix Hotel. Soon they would be out in the open country.

It was nearly a half hour before she turned the pony's head up the winding avenue that led to Ashland. Ashland was the home of Henry Clay, her father's friend and Kentucky's representative in Congress. He was Speaker of the House of Representatives. The Clay family lived in a handsome two-story brick house set back in a rolling woodland.

Mary sprang down from the pony. A small Negro boy appeared from behind the house. Mary tossed him the reins.

She ran up the broad front steps and pulled out the brass bell knob beside the wide ash-wood door. It was opened by a tall Negro man in a black swallow-tailed coat.

Mary looked up at him. "I'd like to see Mr. Clay, please, Charles."

A smile crossed the man's face. "He's busy, Miss Mary. He and Mrs. Clay have guests."

Mary smiled back. "They won't mind seeing me."

She started to push past him. He stretched out a hand to stop her. "Now see here, Miss Mary——"

A man's deep voice spoke from the dining room. "Who is it, Charles?"

"It's Mr. Robert Todd's little daughter, sir."

"Let her come in."

Mary's smile grew broader. "You see, Charles. I told you they wouldn't care."

She went into the house and across the entrance hall. The master of Ashland arose as she entered the dining room. He walked over to meet her and led her to the table. He drew up a chair beside his own. "There, Mary Ann Todd, you shall sit beside me. Would you like that?"

"I'd like it very much, Mr. Clay. Please don't call me Mary Ann, though. Since my little sister Ann Maria came, I'm just Mary." Then she started to climb up in the chair.

With a smile Mrs. Clay leaned forward. "How would you like to go and ask my Jemima to comb those curls? You look hot and tired, child. I am sure you'll find something to wear among our daughters' clothes."

Mary sprang to her feet. A sunny smile spread over her face. She started from the room.

"Hurry back," Mrs. Clay called. "Charles will be serving our dessert soon. It's ice cream."

The unexpected guest stood poised like a bird in the wide archway. There were no signs of temper or naughtiness now on her happy face. She rushed out to find Jemima.

Amused glances went around the table. The four gentlemen from New Orleans were entertained by the uninvited visitor. While they waited for Mary, the conversation continued.

"She comes in to see us quite often," Mrs. Clay said. "We love children. Mary seems fond of us, and we enjoy her."

"A charming little girl," the gentleman on Mr. Clay's left remarked.

"We think so," his host agreed. "Her mother died only a few weeks ago. She left a brood of six children. Two are younger than Mary. Their father has his hands full in spite of the fact that he's a well-to-do young businessman."

"And the Clerk of the General Assembly at Frankfort," a small voice added from the door.

The Clays and their guests turned to look at Mary. In the dainty rose-sprigged muslin frock, she appeared very different from the tousled tomboy she had been a few minutes before.

Mary sat down by Mr. Clay. "My papa writes down all the laws that are made for Kentucky," she told the company gravely.

Charles, bearing a large white-and-gold tureen, appeared at a rear door. The sides of the dish were frosted with moisture.

Mary gave an excited squeal. "Oh, ice cream! We had some on my last birthday. It takes lots of ice to freeze it. But you have loads of it in your icehouse, don't you, Mrs. Clay?" She chattered away.

Outdoors the shadows grew longer. Mrs. Clay was the first to notice this. "It's getting late, Mary. Your Aunt Ann Maria will be worried."

Mary's keen ears had caught the sound of carriage wheels. She laid her napkin on the table and slipped down from her chair. "That must be Nelson coming for me. They guessed where

18

I am." She held out a dimpled hand to her hostess. "Thank you for a lovely time."

The Todd carriage had drawn up at the door. Nelson, in blue broadcloth and brass buttons, sat on the coachman's box. A small Negro boy beside him jumped to the ground. He went back toward the stables. Soon he returned. He was leading Snowball by the reins. He opened the door of the carriage for Mary.

Old Nelson frowned down at her. "Mr. Robert is fit to be tied. Mammy Sally told him that you ran away. I expect you'll get a spanking."

Mary sighed. "Well, it was worth it. I had a wonderful time, with ice cream and everything." Her face broke into a smile. "Thank you for coming to take me home, Nelson. Thank you very much."

A New Adventure

MORE than a year had passed since Mary's runaway visit to Ashland. Her Aunt Ann Maria had left the Todd household. This was a very special day.

"It's almost time for your new mama to be here," Mammy Sally told Mary.

Seven-year-old Mary went on arranging furniture in the dollhouse. If she heard her old nurse, she did not answer.

"Come on, honey," Mammy Sally coaxed. "I still have Ann Maria and little George to dress. Don't you want them to look pretty?"

Mary changed a tiny bed from one room to

another in the dollhouse. "They are the sweetest babies in the whole world," she said.

"Indeed they are," Mammy Sally agreed.

"Is she pretty?" Mary demanded. "Is my stepmother nice?"

The nurse smiled broadly. "Your papa says she is. He told us that he's bringing home a sweet, beautiful mama for you children and a kind mistress for us."

Mary pushed the little furniture back into the dollhouse. "Then I guess I'd better try to look pretty, too." Her eyes sparkled suddenly. "I'll be a moss rose like the picture on our best china. May I wear my rose-colored dress, Mammy? Please say yes."

"Of course you may," the old woman told her.

Mammy Sally went over to a wardrobe and took out a dainty frock. She laid it on a chair and left the room. Mary heard her going down the hall toward the nursery.

Mary unbuttoned her everyday dress and dropped it to the floor. She carefully poured water from the big pitcher into a washbowl. She scrubbed her hands and face. Then she slipped the rose-colored frock over her head.

Suddenly there came to her ears a *thump-thump* from the back yard. She had almost forgotten!

She wriggled the rest of the way into the dress. She ran to the back window. She leaned halfway out. Mammy Sally would have shuddered if she could have seen her.

Yes, they were still there. The well digger and his helper were hard at work.

Mary had been so busy that she had not noticed the men for two days. Now she could hardly believe her eyes. The men had struck an underground stream. They were bringing up very soft mud in their buckets. On the ground it made a growing mass that took up a space almost as large as the kitchen garden. The men dumped another load and lowered the buckets again.

"Lovely *ooshy* stuff!" Mary exclaimed under her breath.

In another minute she was running down the back stairs. She had forgotten her new stepmother, Mammy Sally, and everyone else. All she could think of was that tempting pile of ooze.

Softly Mary stole past the dining room where one of the Todd servants was setting the table. Softly she crept past the kitchen where Chaney was preparing supper.

Mary opened the back door a crack and slid out like a mouse. She gave a sigh of relief as she reached the back yard. Then she glanced toward the upper gallery. There was no sign of Mammy Sally. She looked toward the workmen. Their backs were turned.

How she wished she was barefooted! She could imagine the soft mud pushing up between her toes. But she was in too great a hurry to take off her shoes. She waded into the slippery mass.

Plop-plop-plop! went her feet. It was a task to pick them up and set them down. Now the mud was halfway to her knees. She tried to pick up a handful of the slippery stuff. This was fun. It was like making great big mud pies.

At the front of the house there was the roll of carriage wheels. From a side window Mammy Sally called, "Levi! Elizabeth! Frances! Is Mary with you? Come home, children. Your papa is helping your new mama down from the carriage."

Three children ran out from their Grandmother Parker's house next door. They tore across the wide yard to their own home.

Mary heard nothing. She did not even see her brother and sisters. She was too busy with her new amusement. By this time she was patting the soft mud on her cheeks. It dripped down the front of her rose-colored dress.

The well diggers were the first to see her. One of them wiped his damp forehead on the back of his hand. He turned toward the house. He caught sight of the small figure. "Great jumping Jupiter! Look, Mike!"

The other man turned. His mouth flew open.

25

There was hardly an inch of Mary that was not covered with mud.

At the same moment Levi and the girls burst around one corner of the house. Mammy Sally and Nelson appeared at the other side of it.

Robert Todd stepped out on the long upstairs gallery. His new wife had an arm in his. She looked up at him and said something.

What she said Mr. Todd never knew. He had just caught sight of his fourth child. She was plastered with mud from head to foot.

The roar that burst from his throat could have been heard three blocks away on North Broadway. "Mary Ann Todd!"

The small mud-covered figure looked up from her play. In a flash her happy manner was gone. She was a small copy of her father as she shrieked back, "Robert Smith Todd!"

"Well, there she is," her father said to her stepmother. "And there are the rest of them." He

nodded grimly toward his three oldest children, who were standing openmouthed at the sight of their sister.

Mary wiped the mud off her face. She flashed a smile up to her stepmother. The little girl's dimples were plainly visible.

"I don't usually look this awful, ma'am. I'm sorry I forgot to keep clean. As soon as I wash, I'll be in to see you."

Robert Todd looked darkly from the upstairs porch at his daughter. "And I will see you later in my study," he promised.

A New Friend

OUTSIDE the rain was falling, but the Todd parlor was warm and cheerful. Mary's little stool was drawn up close to her stepmother's big wing chair.

Mary was working on her sampler. Her face was puckered. "I don't like to embroider, Ma," she complained.

"Every little girl makes a sampler," Mrs. Todd told her. "How else would you learn the different stitches? I made a sampler when I was ten years old—just your age."

Mary frowned. Her fingers were hot and sticky. She picked at a stitch. "This old *M* is crooked," she told her mother. "I just can't make my letters as straight as you do."

Mrs. Todd laid baby Margaret in her cradle. She was fast asleep. Her rosebud mouth was slightly open. "Let me see the sampler," Mrs. Todd said.

Mary gladly handed it over. She was tired of sewing. She wished the rain would stop. She wanted to go for a gallop on Snowball. "I'd rather take care of babies than sew," she said, as she bent over little Margaret's cradle.

"Except when they cry," her mother added.

Mary's face turned red. Yesterday she had offered to watch little Margaret. She had seemed like a big doll at first. Then she had begun to fret. Mary had run for Mammy Sally in a hurry.

"Never mind," her mother told her now. "You do very well with babies."

"I like babies," Mary declared. "But I don't see why they must cry so much."

"Or why little girls must be so cross and have temper tantrums," Mrs. Todd replied.

Mary burst out laughing. "All right, Ma. You win. But I just can't help myself. I guess you will see temper tantrums as long as you have me."

Mrs. Todd sighed. "But must you have them so often?"

Mary lowered her eyes. When she raised them again, they were twinkling. "The tantrums don't last long."

"Somebody is always having one. If it isn't you, it's Levi. If it isn't Levi, it's Frances or Elizabeth. Lately even Ann Maria and George have begun."

Mary rocked back and forth. She shook her head like an old woman. "That terrible Todd temper!"

Mrs. Todd laughed in spite of herself. She loved her stepchildren, but sometimes she wished they would be a little more quiet. At times the walls of the house seemed to rock with their shouts, quarrels, and fights. They were a lively bunch.

"It's peaceful with Levi, Frances, and Elizabeth away on a visit," Mary said.

She looked through the door of the little back parlor into the drawing room beyond. Robert Todd had provided a beautiful home for his family. The carpets were rich and soft. The furniture was costly. Family portraits looked down from the walls.

Mary was not thinking about her beautiful home now. The rain beat down on the windows. Some of it even came down the chimney. The fire on the hearth sputtered. Mary's mouth drooped a little.

"It's lonesome without them, too. I'm glad your niece is coming today."

"You are?"

"Yes, ma'am. I have fun with Elizabeth, Frances, and Levi sometimes, but Frances and Elizabeth are always having secrets and whispering in corners. They think they're so grown-up just because they're older than I am. Levi can be nice, but he's too bossy. Ann Maria and George Rogers Clark are too small to count—and Margaret is only a baby."

"So you think you'll like having a playmate your own age?"

"I certainly do. Tell me about Elizabeth Humphreys again."

Mrs. Todd smiled over the sampler at her. "Your father and I felt you needed a companion. I have a niece and namesake who is ten years old. We invited her to come and live with us. She'll attend Dr. Ward's Academy with you."

Mary had heard all this a dozen times, but she was listening eagerly. Her blue eyes were dancing. She clasped her hands excitedly.

"What is she like? Do you think Elizabeth is like me?"

Mrs. Todd thought for a moment. "She has golden hair and brown eyes. She's about as tall as you are. Her home is in Frankfort. Folks there think she is a very nice girl."

"Will she do things?" Mary demanded.

"Do things?" Mrs. Todd repeated in a puzzled way.

"Yes," Mary answered. "Ride horseback, skip rope, climb trees, play Indians. Will she do things like those?"

"Are those the only things you like to do?"

Mary shook her head. "I like to cook when Chaney will let me in the kitchen. I like to make dresses for my dolls. And I love to go out in the carriage with you to make calls."

Mrs. Todd gave her a little pat. "I think you'll find Elizabeth likes the same things you like. She should be here soon."

Outside the rain had stopped. Just as Mrs. Todd spoke, Nelson drove the family carriage up to the hitching block.

"Why, there she is now!" Mrs. Todd said.

Mary rushed to the window. She saw a small girl in a dark-green cloak and a fur-tipped bonnet. She was standing on the sidewalk beside a heap of valises and boxes.

Mary and her mother hurried to the front door.

Mrs. Todd drew the newcomer in and kissed her. "How glad I am to see you, dear!"

Mary and the new girl stood looking at each other. Then Mary put out her hand. "Hello, Elizabeth," she said. "No, I can't call you Elizabeth. That's my sister's name. May I call you Betsy? That's Ma's name and she says you were named for her."

The girl nodded. "I'd like for you to call me Betsy. You must be Mary. Aunt Betsy said her stepdaughter about my age was named Mary."

Soon the two girls were sitting side by side before the fire in the back parlor. The baby was awake and cooing in her cradle. Jane, the Todds' housekeeper, had carried in the big tea tray. Mrs. Todd was cutting slices of rich yellow poundcake. She poured a cup of tea for herself. The girls had hot chocolate.

"Are you glad to be here?" Mary asked Betsy Humphreys.

36

Her new friend spread her fingers before the fire. "Yes. It was a cold drive. Nelson stopped at the forge halfway between here and Frankfort to get a hot brick for my feet."

She looked at Mary. She saw a rosy-cheeked girl with sparkling, mischievous eyes. Then she, too, asked a question. "Are you glad to have me here?"

Mary's answer was quick and certain. "Oh, yes! Gladder than anything!"

"That Old Blabbing Brook"

"PLEASE TELL us your secret," Mary begged Levi.

The Todd children and Betsy Humphreys were playing in Grandma Parker's side yard. It was a bright April day in 1829, just a few months after Betsy had come to live with them. Ma had made them wear their wraps. She believed in being careful.

Levi smiled in a teasing way at the others. "You'll find out in plenty of time. Mary, for a ten-year-old girl you have a lot of curiosity."

"Tell us," Mary insisted.

"Yes, do," Betsy begged.

Elizabeth and Frances said nothing. They knew how Levi loved to tease.

"If you want to learn my secret, you'll have to go with me to that red-brick house down on Main Street—the fine one that comes right down to the sidewalk and has so much ground around it. You know the one I mean, don't you?"

Elizabeth and Frances nodded. They, too, wondered what Levi had planned for them.

"We're ready," Betsy told him.

"Wait a minute," Mary said.

She ran toward the rear of the house. In a short time she came back leading her pony, Snowball.

Levi scowled. "I planned to cut through the Baptist churchyard. We'll be certain to meet Pa if we go around by Broadway. He'll want to know all about where we're going. Now you have that old pony, so we can't go through the churchyard."

"Snowball can go anywhere you can," Mary told him quickly.

"Down the stone steps?"

"Wait and see."

The girls and Levi started across the street. They walked slowly. Down by the board fence Mary discovered a tiny blue flower. She stooped to pick it.

"It's a violet!" she exclaimed. "The first one I've seen this spring."

"Oh, come on!" Levi urged. "Why must girls always stop to pick flowers?"

"I love flowers," Mary protested. "Why shouldn't I pick them?"

"Ma loves them, too," Elizabeth said. "She's always wishing our house had a larger conservatory, or some other special place for growing flowers."

"That house on Main Street has a conservatory," Mary said.

"It has something else, too," Levi told her with a grin.

"What?" Mary demanded.

"Never you mind. Little girls shouldn't ask questions. You'll soon find out."

By now the children were walking down the stone steps that went from the church to the street. Mary led Snowball down the rolling lawn. The grass was easier than the stones on the pony's feet.

Now they were ready to go out the little iron gate, but Snowball refused. She stood stock-still. She could not jump the fence. She must walk down several of the stone steps.

"Now what?" Levi demanded. "She's so fat we'll never get her through that gate even if we persuade her to go down the steps. I guess we'll have to starve her for a couple of days."

"You will not," Mary retorted. "That gate is plenty wide enough. Come on, Snowball."

Snowball would not budge. Mary tugged
at the reins. Still Snowball refused to move. She
stood like a rock. The children looked at one
another.

"I have an idea," Levi said suddenly.

He ran toward the little alley at the east side of the churchyard. There was a blacksmith's shop on the steep hill that led up to Short Street.

Soon Levi came back. He was carrying a long stick. One end of it was blazing. He had lighted it at the blacksmith's forge. "She'll move if I touch her hoofs with this."

"No!" Mary stepped between him and the pony. "Don't you dare! I won't let you hurt my darling Snowball. Don't come an inch closer!"

Perhaps Snowball saw the flaming stick in Levi's hand. Perhaps she was startled by Mary's anger. At any rate, she set her little hoofs down on the hard stones. She picked her way daintily down to the gate and out onto the sidewalk.

"There," Mary said. "You can't drive her. She's like me. She'll move when she's good and ready—not before."

They saw the red-brick house farther down the street. The spacious grounds on either side were dotted with trees and shrubs. It was one of the prettiest places in Lexington.

"Let's steal around back," Levi said mysteriously. "No one in the house must see us here."

Elizabeth and Frances exchanged glances. What was Levi up to now?

Mary and Betsy fell in with his plan. Mary wrapped Snowball's reins firmly about her hand. She advanced on tiptoe. "We must stay hidden," she whispered to the other girls. "Go to the left of those lilac bushes. Then we won't be seen."

Elizabeth and Frances followed good-humoredly. Although they were only a year or so older, they felt sometimes as though Mary, Betsy, and Levi were mere children.

Presently they came out at the foot of the lilac bushes. They were now deep in the garden and completely hidden from the house. A small stream rippled and tumbled the length of the grounds.

44

Mary gave a squeal of delight and let go of Snowball's reins. "I knew there was a brook back here, but I didn't know it was so wide or so deep."

Levi pulled off his boots. "We'll go wading before Pa tells us it's too early in the spring."

"Do you think we should?" Frances asked. "Ma hasn't let us take off our winter underwear yet."

Mary was dabbling her little white feet in the water. Her shoes and stockings lay on the grass. She rolled her long woolen underwear up to her knees.

"Hateful stuff! It scratches," she fussed. Her blue eyes were dancing as she looked up at the others. "Besides, if we wait for permission to change to summer things or to go wading, we won't get it before the Fourth of July."

Soon all the children were knee-deep in the chilly water. For more than an hour they played.

Frances and Elizabeth forgot their grown-up ways. They played as heartily as Mary, Betsy, and Levi. They sailed boats made of sticks. They built dams. They had water fights.

Suddenly Mary slipped on a mossy stone and tumbled headlong into the water. She picked

herself up and stretched out on the sunny bank near Snowball. She was laughing so hard she could hardly speak.

"Ugh! You look like a drowned rat," Levi said.

"Hurry home," Elizabeth advised. "You must change your clothes so you won't catch a cold."

"You sound like Ma," Mary told her. "I hope I can creep in without her sharp eye discovering me."

"Haven't we had fun?" Frances sighed.

Mary nodded. "Enough fun to make a cold worth while. I never had such a good time in my whole life."

"That's what you said when you waded in the mud from the well," Levi reminded her.

Mary rose with dignity. "I always have a good time, no matter what I'm doing." She held her head high as they returned home.

That evening the Todds were gathered around

the table for their evening meal. All the children except the two smaller babies were present. They were fast asleep upstairs. Mr. Todd was at the head of the long table. He unfolded his napkin.

"And I said to Mr. Clay—" he remarked to his wife.

"Ker-choo!" Mary muffled the sneeze in the depths of her napkin. Levi and the girls stared guiltily at her.

"—that I feel the Whig party is growing stronger every day——"

"Ker-choo!"

This time Mary was too late to hide the sneeze. It blasted the calm of the quiet dining room. Betsy giggled. Levi raised his eyebrows.

"You must be taking cold, dear," their stepmother said.

At that moment Mammy Sally appeared in the doorway. She had a dark look on her face.

48

Without a word she held up the soaking dress which Mary had worn when she fell into the creek. "I found it in Miss Mary's closet," she told Mrs. Todd.

"Mary Ann Todd, have you been wading?" her father asked.

She turned wide eyes toward him. "Of course, Pa. How else could my dress have become wet? That old *blabbing* brook! I might have known it would tell on me."

"You deserve to be punished," Mr. Todd said, "but I guess the misery of having a cold will be punishment enough."

The Little
Railroad

MARY LOOKED into the window of Monsieur Giron's confectionery. She had ten cents in her small beaded purse. It was a whole week's allowance. Should she buy two of the tempting little spice cakes? Should she save her money for another day? She could not decide.

Someone touched her arm. She looked up. Mr. Henry Clay was looking down at her.

Mary broke into a big smile. "Mr. Clay! I thought you were in Washington."

"I was," he told her. "But, you know, I come back once in a while. What are you doing so far from home?"

"Everyone except me has measles," Mary answered cheerfully. "I expect I shall come down with them any day now."

"Keep away from me!" Henry Clay urged jokingly. "I don't want them."

Mary burst out laughing. "I thought all grown-ups had already had them."

"I had measles when I was a little boy back in Virginia," Mr. Clay confessed. "I didn't enjoy them at all."

"I think I might enjoy them," Mary said. "Someone rocks the small children from morning till night. Pa reads stories to Levi and Ann Maria every minute he's home. Ma and Mammy Sally run upstairs and downstairs with pillows and trays and pitchers of lemonade. Nobody pays any attention to a well person, so I came out for a walk."

"Nobody pays any attention to me either," Mr. Clay complained. "My wife is busy making preserves. All my boys and girls are young men and women. They're too busy to amuse their poor old father. I wish I knew someone about ten years old."

Mary looked quickly at him. His face was sober, but his bright, blue eyes were twinkling.

Mary danced up and down with excitement. "I'm ten years old. We could amuse each other."

"We certainly could," he agreed. "I have a suggestion."

"What is it?"

"I will tell you later," he said with a mysterious air. "First, let's go into the shop of our French friend here."

He opened the door for her. Mary entered with a hop, a skip, and a jump.

Monsieur Giron came to meet them. He was so round and plump that he seemed to bounce as he walked. He wore a neat pointed little beard. He spoke with a French accent.

"Mr. Clay and little Miss Todd!" he exclaimed as he made a sweeping bow. "I am happy to welcome you to my establishment."

Mary smiled in spite of herself. She liked the little man, but his foreign manners sometimes amused her.

"Mary and I feel the need of refreshment," Mr. Clay told Monsieur Giron. "Which of your delightful creations do you especially recommend?"

The fat little Frenchman clasped his hands and rolled his eyes toward the ceiling. "They are all perfect!" he announced.

"Ze goodies are all light as air, ze texture of an angel's wing, sweet as honey in ze comb. Ze sweets for ze sweet child——"

Mary interrupted him. By now her face was pressed to the high glass counter. "Those little spice cakes?" she asked Mr. Clay.

Monsieur Giron continued. "Ze spice cakes

—ze almond macaroons—ze tiny cream puffs
—ze eclairs—ze petit fours——"

"The little spice cakes iced with caramel," Mr.
Clay said firmly.

Mary's head swam at the sight of so many
goodies. She was glad Mr. Clay was there to
order for her.

Soon she and the tall statesman were out on the sidewalk again. She held a brown paper cone in her hand. The cakes were in the cone. She looked back at the small Frenchman in the doorway of the shop.

"*Au revoir, Monsieur,*" she called. "Good-by, sir."

"You have a real Parisian accent, Mary," her companion said.

She gave a sigh. "Now I know you're only teasing me. I want so much to learn to speak French. Do you suppose I ever shall?"

Mr. Clay nodded. "Of course. You can do anything if you want to enough. Take me, for example. I want to be President of the United States. I intend to be some day. There's only one thing I want more."

"What's that?"

"To be right in my thinking and acting."

Mary hardly heard him. She had stopped with

a cupcake halfway to her mouth. "I forgot. Ma says a lady never eats on the street."

Mr. Clay laughed. "You aren't a lady yet. You're only a little girl."

Mary still looked worried. "But Ma says I should be ladylike in my ways."

Mr. Clay nodded. "Your mother is right. I'll tell you what we'll do. We'll compromise."

"Compromise?"

"Yes. We'll eat our cake quickly before we get to Main Street. There's no one to see us here."

Mary was happy again. Mr. Clay's suggestion seemed very sensible. They walked along together and munched at their cakes.

When they reached the town pump, they stopped. Mary pushed the long handle up and down several times. The clear water flowed from the mouth of the pump. She and Mr. Clay washed their sticky hands. He drew a white linen handkerchief from his vest pocket. They used it for a towel.

Now they were walking east on Main Street. They passed the Phoenix Hotel. Several men were sitting in chairs at the edge of the sidewalk.

"Are we going to walk all the way to Ashland?" Mary asked.

He shook his head. "That's too far. We'll turn at Rose Street and go down toward the Town Branch, which runs along Water Street. I want to show you something interesting."

Before long they reached a long red-brick building on the banks of the Town Branch. Over the door was a sign. Mary read it aloud:

"T. BARLOW."

"Mr. Barlow is a friend of mine," Henry Clay told her. "He's a very smart fellow. You'll agree when you see what he has made."

He led her into a barnlike interior. Rough stairs led up to the second floor. On the ground floor Mary caught a glimpse of a huge machine and dozens of small kegs. Several of them were open. They held quantities of nails.

Mr. Clay looked at them. "Barlow is an inventor," he told her. "This kind of nail has al-

most replaced the old wooden pegs which carpenters once used."

He was nearly upstairs by now. Mary hurried after him.

She heard a grinding noise and a *chug-chug-chug*. What could those sounds be?

Now she and Mr. Clay had reached the upper floor. From the hallway they stepped into a long room. Mary caught her breath. She could scarcely believe her eyes.

A large oval track made of wood circled the room. A small coach stood on the rails. It looked like the Todd carriage except that it lacked a coachman's seat. In front of the coach was a strange thing on wheels, like nothing Mary had ever seen before.

A tall man was bending over the mysterious contraption. He turned a screw driver. He got aboard and touched a lever.

Puff-puff-puff! Chug-chug-chug!

The odd machine and the little coach began to move forward on the tracks. With an open mouth Mary watched them rolling along. Nothing in sight was pushing or pulling them. "It just can't be!" she announced.

Then it stopped and Mr. Barlow got off. The men laughed heartily at Mary's amazement.

"Someday a locomotive like this, but much bigger, will draw coaches with passengers in them all the way to Frankfort, the capital of our state," Mr. Clay told her.

She looked closely at her friend. He was serious.

"Would you like to ride behind my locomotive?" Mr. Barlow asked.

Mary's eyes sparkled. "Will you ride with me?" she asked Mr. Clay.

He shook his head. "The engine isn't powerful enough to pull both of us, but it will pull two children."

60

"Here's a lad," Mr. Barlow said. He nodded toward a boy about Mary's age who had just carried a heavy coil of wire into the room. "Tim is my helper. He knows how to start and stop the engine."

The boy came forward eagerly. His clothes were patched and worn, but he was neat and clean. His eyes shone with excitement. Mary recognized him at once. He was the eldest of a large family who lived on the outskirts of town. His mother took in washing and worked from morning till night. His father held no regular job and had been arrested more than once for being a troublemaker.

Tim bent over the locomotive. His fingers moved skillfully among the little levers and controls.

"May I be a passenger?" Mary asked him.

He straightened up. "Indeed you may," he smilingly told her.

He helped her into the tiny coach. Then he
looked toward Mr. Barlow. The inventor smiled
and nodded.

Tim leaned forward and pushed down on a
lever. The engine and coach moved slowly along
the tracks.

"O-o-h, what fun!" Mary squealed.

"Look at them," Mr. Clay said proudly. "The daughter of one of the richest men in town and the son of the town's ne'er-do-well. They represent democracy. Those two wouldn't be riding together in any other country in the world. They are living bits of America."

Mr. Barlow added. "You're right, Henry, and the girl is a fine lass. I prophesy she'll choose a man someday for his ability and not for his wealthy or famous ancestors."

Hoop Skirts

MARY AND Betsy sat on the floor in the upper
hall at the head of the stairs. No one could see
them from below, but the girls had a perfect
view of all that went on. Mr. and Mrs. Todd
were having a reception—one of the first this
fall.

Before Mrs. Todd went downstairs, she had
stopped in the girls' bedroom.

"Oh, you look pretty!" Mary exclaimed, sitting up in bed. "In that lovely pink silk you look
prettier than any of the pretty ladies in the fash-
ion books."

"Thank you, Mary," her mother said. "You

and Betsy look as though you had stepped out of a storybook."

"Which one?" the girls asked in one breath.

"Grimm's *Fairy Tales*," she told them. "Mary with her rosy cheeks, reminds me of Rose Red. Now Betsy, with her golden plaits and milk-white skin, is more like Snow White."

"I'd rather go downstairs than look like Rose Red," Mary said wistfully.

Mrs. Todd leaned over to give the girls a good-night kiss. "All that will come later," she told them. "You're only ten years old."

They heard her rustling down the hall. Mary sprang from the bed. "If we can't go down, at least we can watch them," she told Betsy.

"Do you think we dare?" Betsy asked.

"Of course," Mary answered. "What possible harm can come of it?"

They made their way to the hall and seated themselves in the shadows. With wide-open eyes they stared between the rails. Down below, ladies with swaying hoop skirts were moving gracefully to and fro. Gentlemen in swallow-tailed coats walked beside them. Old Nelson bore a silver tray of iced punch.

Mary rose to her feet. She swayed back and forth in the shadows. Pretending she was one of the ladies, Mary tried to imitate the steps of the dance and tripped on her long nightgown.

She grinned at her awkwardness and jumped quickly to her feet again.

Betsy doubled over in silent laughter.

"I simply must have a skirt with hoops!" Mary told her.

Betsy kept on giggling. "I can imagine what Aunt will say if you ask her for one. Sh-h, Mary! Someone downstairs will hear you. Then we'll be sent off to bed in a hurry."

Mary started to dance again. Then she stopped for a moment. One bare foot was in the air. Her eyes were bright with mischief. "We will have them!" she declared. "We will have them by Sunday. We'll wear hoop skirts to Sunday school and make the preacher's eyes pop out of his head."

Betsy giggled again. "How awful!"

"Never fear," Mary promised. "The hoop skirts are as good as ours."

The next day was Saturday. Early in the morning Mary took a large market basket and slipped out the back way.

"Don't you dare tell anyone where I am," she cautioned Betsy. "You can't, anyhow, because you don't know where I'm going. Better for you not to know if anyone asks you where I am. But you can count on what I said, 'We'll have our hoop skirts for Sunday school tomorrow.' "

With Mary gone the house seemed very still. Betsy wandered from room to room. She looked at the Todd family portraits in their gold-leaf frames.

Three Todd men looked down at her. They were Levi, Robert, and John. Levi was the Todd children's grandfather. Robert and John were their great-uncles. All three had been early Kentucky pioneers.

Eliza Parker Todd, Mary's own mother, smiled down at Betsy. The girl in the portrait was young and beautiful. Mary would look like her someday, Betsy thought, but Mary had already a fire and a glow that the girl in the portrait lacked.

Betsy turned away from the pictures. With one finger she picked out a tune on the spinet. She was careful to keep away from Mrs. Todd, who was in the conservatory tending the night-blooming cereus. She didn't want to be questioned.

At last she heard quick steps in the center hall. She turned in time to see Mary stealing softly up the stairs. She still carried the market basket. It was filled with long willow switches.

Mary put a finger to her lips. Both girls looked in the direction of the conservatory.

Mary beckoned to Betsy. The girls crept softly up to their bedroom. Safe at last, Mary turned the key in the lock. She pointed to the switches in the basket. "Mrs. Hostetter gave them to me. They'll make frames for our hoop skirts."

"Does she know what you mean to do with them?"

Mary laughed. "I think she somehow got the idea that Ma wants to use them on Levi. She seemed very happy to give them to me. She doesn't care much for Levi since he gave her old cat a ride in the well bucket."

She drew down her mouth and looked so much like Mrs. Hostetter that Betsy squealed with glee.

"Sh-h!" Mary said. "Let's go to the sewing room and take a look at Ma's hoop-skirt frame."

They unlocked the door and tiptoed down the hall. Inside the small sewing room they examined with interest the wire frame which Ma wore under her hoop skirts.

"It looks complicated," Betsy said. "Maybe we should make our frames of wire, too."

"And where would we get wire, and what would we cut it with?" Mary asked. "Levi guards his tools day and night. Besides, these willow switches will bend easier. See?" She placed a long willow switch along the big bell-like frame.

Betsy still looked puzzled. "No, I don't see, but I'm sure you can do it if anyone can, Mary."

They went back to the bedroom. Once more they locked the door. Then Mary opened the door of the wardrobe and took down the white muslin dresses which they always wore on Sunday. "Let's get to work. With luck we should make a good start before supper."

Both girls bent over the dresses. The skirts were full of gathers at the waist. Mary turned the frocks inside out. She bent one of the limber switches in an arc. "There! They will be just like real hoops."

Betsy was not certain that she understood, but she trusted Mary. "Just tell me what to do and I'll do it," she promised.

The girls began to sew the switches to the skirts. Soon the floor was littered with scraps of willow. The frames grew slowly. The task made their fingers sore, but they did not give up.

"It's getting late," Betsy said. She was looking out the window at the long shadows in the flower garden.

Downstairs the supper bell rang loudly. Mary sprang to her feet. "Let's go," she told Betsy. "We don't want anyone coming up here to look for us."

The two girls walked into the dining room. The other members of the family were already seated.

"What have you been up to?" Levi asked Mary. "You look like the cat that ate the canary."

"Be quiet, children," Robert Todd said. "Bow your heads."

Mary turned up her nose and stuck out her tongue at Levi, under cover of her napkin. He made a face at her. Mary felt her mother looking at her. She closed her eyes and bowed her head.

After supper Mary wiggled and squirmed in the drawing room. She pretended to hide a yawn behind her hand. "I'm sleepy, Ma," she said. "If you'll excuse me, I think I'll go upstairs."

"So soon?" Mrs. Todd asked in surprise.

"Yes, ma'am. Aren't you tired, too, Betsy?"

"Yes," Betsy agreed. "Yes, I am."

The girls made their escape to the upper floor. With difficulty they hid their laughter.

Mary drew the key from her pinafore pocket. She turned the key in the lock. Then the girls set straight to work again.

"When we hear the family coming, we'll blow out the candles and leap into bed," Mary said.

For the most part the girls were very happy with the results they were getting. Still the hoop skirts were not finished. There were bunches and knots here and there. The evening sped by.

They could hardly believe their ears when they heard the family in the downstairs hall. The others were about to come up.

"Quick!" Mary whispered.

She tumbled out of her clothes. Betsy did the same. Mary snuffed out the candles. The girls jumped into bed.

They heard Mr. Todd's heavy tread on the stairs. Suddenly Mary leaped out of bed. The moonlight was shining in at the windows. She could see objects in the room plainly. She threw the dresses behind a big chair. She kicked the willow switches under the chair. Then she bounced back into bed.

Mr. Todd went past their door. The girls were shaking with glee. Mrs. Todd and the older girls spoke in low tones as they passed Mary and Betsy's door. Levi went whistling down the hall to his room. The younger Todds had been in bed for hours.

For a long time the two plotters lay without saying a word. At last the house was still. Not a sound could be heard.

Mary stole out of bed. She lighted the candles. "Get up," she whispered to Betsy. "We must finish our hoop skirts."

Far into the night the two girls sewed until finally the dresses were ready to wear.

Sunday dawned clear and bright. In the Todd household there was the usual bustle of getting ready for church and Sunday school. Mary almost swallowed her breakfast whole. She frowned at Betsy, who was still eating an egg. "Don't poke so!" she said.

"Why, Mary, I never knew you to be in such a hurry for Sunday school," Mrs. Todd said.

Mary flashed her a smile. "I never was."

The next half hour went by on wings. Mary and Betsy finished dressing. They put on their homemade hoop skirts. No imports from Paris were ever more admired. Betsy lingered to add a few finishing touches.

Mary was dressed and waiting in front of the house on the sidewalk when Betsy came out the front door. She minced up and down for the benefit of the admiring Betsy. Both girls were in their glory.

From behind them came a deep chuckle and a soft laugh. The girls whirled round. Mr. Todd stood framed in the door. He looked very handsome in his black Sunday broadcloth coat and tall silk hat. He carried his gold-headed cane under his arm. Mrs. Todd in shimmering gray silk stood beside him. Her eyes were dancing with laughter.

Mr. Todd's voice shook with amusement. "Go put on something more suitable for your years, my little peacocks."

Mary's eyes filled with tears. She looked sadly at Betsy. Their plans had failed. Their hopes were dashed. She gave a sniffle as she ran into the house past her parents.

At the foot of the stairs Levi was waiting. He bowed, then held out a long willow switch. "For my lady," he said with a grin. "I think I know where Ma ought to use it on you."

Mary stamped her foot. "You're mean! I'll have hoops one of these days. Wait and see. I'll be a fine lady with the prettiest clothes in the whole world."

"Fine feathers don't always make fine birds," Levi said.

Surprise from New Orleans

"THE LAST time Pa saw me I was only ten years old," Mary told the family at the breakfast table.

"You've been eleven only two weeks," Levi reminded her, "and Pa has been gone only three."

Mary looked a little sad. "It seems as though he has been gone forever."

"I was saving this news for a surprise. Your father will be home from New Orleans today," Mrs. Todd told the children.

There were happy cries from the children. Little Ann Maria and George looked as pleased as the older ones.

"There he is now!" Mary exclaimed.

She had caught a glimpse out the window of her father getting down from the Todd carriage. Nelson was laden with boxes and packages enough to contain presents for the entire family.

All the young Todds and Betsy Humphreys rushed to the front door. They surrounded Robert Todd with a shower of hugs and kisses.

"The stagecoach was early," he told his wife over the heads of the excited youngsters.

"None too early," she answered with a smile. "We've missed you. I know you'll be glad to hear that the children have been unusually good. Mary has made a special effort."

"Has she?" He turned toward Mary. She grew red with pleasure. He looked at all the children. There was really a houseful of Todds.

His wife went on talking. "When Mammy Sally was busy, Mary took care of little Margaret for me."

Mr. Todd's eyes twinkled. "No show of the Todd temper?"

Mary looked up quickly. He was laughing. Sometimes the Todd temper was a nuisance, but at other times it was a joke. At any rate, Mary knew that she and her father had more than their share of it.

"Well-l, not too much," his wife said.

"We must see what I have for Mary. She may be growing up at last. Let's go to the little back parlor. Nelson took my plunder there."

The family sat in a big circle. Everyone looked eagerly at Robert Todd. He sat in a big wing chair. He was surrounded by boxes and packages. "For her good behavior Mary shall be my messenger," he declared.

Mary skipped to his side. The first box he handed her was a long narrow one wrapped in tissue paper and ribbons. "For your mother," he said.

Mrs. Todd opened the box. The children crowded about her. A beautiful necklace of pearls was lying on the white satin. There was a chorus of "Oh's!" and "Ah's!"

Elizabeth and Frances received similar boxes. Their gifts were lovely coral necklaces. There were books for Levi, and toys and trinkets for the younger Todds. For everybody to share, there was a large box of clear-colored candies molded in the shapes of little animals, flowers, and fruits.

"Now, Mary, it's your turn and Betsy's," her father told her. He handed each of the girls a large square box. "I seem to remember something about hoop skirts."

Mary looked at Betsy. "They couldn't be hoop skirts," she whispered. "The boxes aren't large enough."

They tore off the wrapping and lifted the tops from the boxes.

"Oh!" gasped Mary.

"Oh!" breathed Betsy.

"No, they aren't hoop skirts," Robert Todd agreed, "but I hope you'll enjoy the frocks the material will make. When you are old enough for hoop skirts, you shall have them."

Under the tissue paper in each box lay fold after fold of beautiful sheer, hand-embroidered pink muslin.

"I love it!" Mary told her father. "I'll wear it until there isn't a scrap left. I don't mind waiting for my hoops now."

"It came from one of the finest shops in New Orleans," Mr. Todd said. "Now open your other packages."

Mary and Betsy lost no time in tearing off the paper from their second gifts. Again there was a chorus of delight. Each girl had a beautiful French doll.

"Press on them," Mr. Todd told the girls.

"Ma-ma!" the china babies squeaked.

Mary closed her eyes happily and drew a deep breath. "I missed you a lot, Pa, but I wish you could come home from New Orleans every day."

A little later Mary went to the kitchen to show her treasures to their beloved cook Chaney.

Chaney's seven-year old granddaughter Dinah was seated on a tall stool by the table. Dinah and her parents were slaves of a lady who lived on South Broadway Hill. Dinah was watching her grandmother roll out pastry for blackberry pies.

"I didn't know you were here, Di," Mary said.

"Her mistress sent her all the way here to get a recipe from me," Chaney said proudly.

"Wait a minute," Mary told the little Negro girl.

She rushed back to the parlor and took a double handful of candies from the box. In a minute she was back in the kitchen. She dropped the candies on the table beside Di.

"For me?" the delighted child exclaimed. "I never saw anything so pretty in my life."

Mary was overjoyed to see Di so happy. Without stopping to think, she picked up her new French doll and placed it in Di's arms.

The child stared at the gift. Her mouth

opened wide in surprise. Old Chaney shook her head in disapproval.

A voice spoke from the doorway. "You can't do that, Mary."

Mary whirled about to meet her mother's quiet gaze.

"It's my doll," Mary objected.

"Your father brought it all the way from New Orleans for you. I believe he'd feel hurt if he knew you wanted to give it away."

Di held out the doll to Mary. Her eyes were full of tears. Mary was unhappy, too.

"I know I shouldn't have done it. But I want Di to be happy. May I give her my other doll?"

Mrs. Todd hesitated. Then she nodded.

Mary ran out of the room. Before long she returned with a dainty doll in a blue dress. She laid it in Di's arms. "I shouldn't have given away the doll Pa had just brought me. I hope you like this one just as much."

Di nodded. She was already hugging her dolly close and singing it a little song.

Mary danced out the door. She still had her doll from New Orleans. Di was satisfied. Everything was all right once more.

"Bless her little heart!" Old Chaney said softly. "I believe Miss Mary would give away her head if it wasn't fastened to her shoulders."

An Indian Scare

THE TODD carriage was rolling down the dusty Richmond turnpike. Old Nelson on the coachman's box looked down toward his noisy passengers once in a while. Then he smiled and looked back at the road.

Inside the carriage were Mary, Levi, and little Ann Maria. They were on their way to their Uncle Robert Stuart's house at Walnut Hills. During the winter months he lived with his large family in Lexington. He taught languages at Transylvania College. In the summer the Stuarts moved to the country.

"We're almost there!" Mary cried. She forgot

that she was now twelve years old. She bounced up and down with excitement. Levi thrust his head out the window. Little Ann Maria climbed up on the seat. Her yellow curls bobbed up and down. "I want to see, too," she exclaimed.

The big white house stood on a hill. It was surrounded by tall forest trees. A brook ran through the meadow beside it. The little stone church was on a nearby knoll. The church faced a side road that led off the Richmond turnpike.

Now they were leaving the hot dusty road. Nelson had turned the horses up a winding avenue. Margaret and John Todd Stuart were waiting beside the hitching block for their cousins to arrive.

Nelson drew the reins. The horses stopped. The young Todds climbed out.

"I thought you'd never come," Margaret Stuart said to Mary.

John Stuart said nothing. He grinned at Levi.

There was promise of hunting, fishing, and exploring in that look.

The Todd children's aunt and uncle came out the front door. They were glad to see their visitors. Two small Stuarts took over Ann Maria at once.

Old Nelson raised his hat as he started the carriage around the circle. "Mr. Todd told me to come back for the children Monday," he called to Mr. and Mrs. Stuart. Then he drove away.

Mary smiled up at her aunt and uncle. "I always feel as though I've come to a magic world when I come to Walnut Hills."

Her Uncle Robert patted her head. "How would you like to begin with a visit to Elk Lick Falls?"

The boys and the girls clapped their hands. It was their favorite picnic spot.

Before long all the Stuarts and the three young Todds were riding off in a big farm wagon. They wore old clothes. They carried a big picnic basket filled with good things to eat.

"I wish I could live out here forever," Mary declared.

"You'd soon get bored," Levi reminded her. "You'd miss your old dancing class."

"Do you like to dance?" Aunt Mary asked her.

Levi did not give her time to answer. "She and a lot of other silly girls take dancing lessons from Monsieur Xaupi every Monday afternoon."

"Do any of the boys take lessons?" Uncle Robert asked slyly.

Levi's face grew red. "Only a few sissies. None of my friends do."

The grownups laughed. "Just wait a few years, my boy," Uncle Robert told him.

"I know why Mary likes the lessons so well," Levi went on. "Monsieur Giron's confectionery is in the same building, that's why."

"He makes the most beautiful cakes," Mary declared. "You should see them. They have roses of spun sugar and icing two inches thick. Um-m-m!"

"I'm sure Levi likes the sweetshop even if he doesn't care for dancing," Aunt Mary said.

"I love dancing!" Mary exclaimed. "Monsieur Xaupi is so nice, and Monsieur Giron is a dear little man just five feet high. They're teaching me to speak French. I can say *'Bon soir.'* That's 'Good evening.' And *'Parlez-vous francais?'* That's 'Do you speak French?' But I like dancing best of all."

She stood up in the wagon and twirled about on one foot.

"Suppose you dance down to the ground," Uncle Robert told her. He drew the reins and brought the big horses to a standstill. "Here we are. Climb out, children."

They were in a wide grassy meadow that

stretched as far as they could see on either side. At the far end it took a sudden turn down toward Elk Lick Creek. Uncle Robert told them that the creek flowed into the Kentucky River a few miles farther on.

When they reached the falls, Mrs. Stuart spread a cloth on the ground for their lunch. The children eagerly unpacked the baskets of food. Margaret set out the fried chicken. Betsy put on the flaky biscuits and dill pickles. John carried the heavy ripe watermelon from the wagon while Levi brought the big stone jar of cold sweet milk. Mary's mouth watered as she set the tempting chocolate cake in the center of the cloth.

"This spot was not so peaceful long ago when elk and other animals came down to lick the salt in the rocks," Uncle Robert said, looking toward the creek.

Mary looked at the creek's rippling falls. They

were only a few yards away. She could imagine Indians paddling down the wide stream in their canoes. They must have carried their boats around the steep falls.

"I'm glad I didn't live then," she said with a shiver.

"Girls are scaredy-cats," Levi declared.

"Mary would be brave if she had to," Uncle Robert put in. "You children don't come from people who frighten easily. If they were scared, they met whatever came and did their duty."

"Your father also is a brave man," Mrs. Stuart told the Todd children. "He was determined to go off to war in 1812 although he was only a boy. He had several narrow escapes, but at last he came home."

"And your other brothers were fighters, too," Robert Stuart reminded his wife. "John barely escaped with his life in that war. Sam was a captive of the Indians for more than a year. Then peace came, and they were safe once more after all their days of living in danger."

"And here we are on the banks of Elk Lick Creek where Indians once roamed," Aunt Mary finished.

Then Mr. Stuart brushed the crumbs from his lap. "I must go to see a man who lives a mile or so down the road." He stood up.

"I'll go with you," his wife told him. "Margaret, you and Mary take good care of the smaller children."

Mary watched the grownups disappear over the top of the hill. Levi and John soon wandered down the creek and off into the woods. Mary and Margaret were left alone with the three small children.

Mary had eaten a big lunch. The day was hot. The place was still. She dozed off. Suddenly she was awakened by a frightened cry from her cousin. "Mary!"

She sat up and rubbed her eyes. Her first fear was that Ann Maria or one of the little Stuarts had fallen into deep water.

Margaret's face was white. She was pointing straight ahead. Mary saw them, too. Around the bend came five Indians bedecked in blankets and feathers.

Margaret snatched up a little brother under each arm. Then she turned and started up the steep slope in the direction of the turnpike.

Mary looked wildly about her. Little Ann Maria was playing on the sunny slope between her and the Indians.

Her heart was in her mouth. For a moment she could not move. Then she dashed toward her little sister.

The Indians came nearer. Mary remembered all the horrible frontier tales she had ever heard. Would two more Todds be added to the list of victims?

She looked toward the steep bank. Ann Maria was too heavy a child for Mary to carry that far.

The Indians came steadily on, in single file. Mary stood her ground. Her teeth were chattering, but her stubborn chin went out. She tossed her head. Ann Maria was crying now.

Mary stamped her foot. "Don't you dare touch my little sister!" she commanded.

The Indians stopped. They were almost close enough now to touch the girls.

Mary forgot her own fear. All the Todd temper showed in her face. She hugged Ann Maria close to her. "Aren't you ashamed to scare a tiny girl like her?" she exclaimed.

The Indians stood without saying a word. They looked down at the girls. Suddenly Mary heard a welcome voice behind her cry, "Red Wolf!"

Her uncle was hurrying down the steep bank. There was a smile on his face. He did not seem at all alarmed.

The tall Indian at the head of the group stepped forward. Robert Stuart laid a friendly hand on his shoulder.

The Indian pointed to Mary. A slight smile crossed his face.

Robert Stuart turned to his nieces. There were still tears on Ann Maria's face. Mary was shaking with fear. Their uncle looked worried.

"Children! I'm sorry if these fellows frightened you. They have come down from the mountains. They are on their way to Frankfort. They go there each summer to get new blankets and a small sum of money. It's little enough when you remember that their ancestors once owned this land."

Mary bit her lips. "It's all right, but I thought at first they intended to scalp us."

Robert Stuart laughed and Red Wolf allowed the ghost of a smile to play about his lips. Again he pointed at Mary. He said just two words, "Brave girl."

The Journey to Frankfort

"BE GOOD girls," Mrs. Todd called to Mary and her niece Betsy.

"We will," the departing travelers promised. "Don't worry Grandmother Humphreys."

"We won't," they chorused.

Inside the carriage the girls exchanged happy glances. At last they were rolling down the Frankfort turnpike on their way to Grandmother Humphreys' house twenty-six miles away. This was Mary's first trip to Betsy's home town. She had looked forward to the day for weeks.

"I never thought I'd be allowed to make such a long journey," Mary said.

"Isn't it wonderful?" Betsy asked her. "I feel as grown-up as though I were in my teens instead of just twelve, don't you?"

"Of course."

It was a long hot journey. The girls grew tired and sleepy. They dozed in the carriage. The big fat horses trotted slowly.

At last they came to the top of a high, steep hill. Down in the valley lay the Kentucky River.

The roofs of many houses showed between the treetops.

Mary looked at Betsy. Her eyes were still closed. Mary leaned over and shook her. "Wake up!"

Betsy sat up and rubbed her eyes. She looked down the hill. A smile came over her face. "It's Frankfort," she announced. "We're nearly home."

Soon the carriage drove up to an old red-brick house with tall white pillars. Nelson stopped the horses. He climbed down and opened the door of the carriage for Mary and Betsy.

The girls went up the flagged walk. Nelson followed with the luggage. A sweet-faced lady with white hair stood in the doorway. She wore a lace cap and a gown of shimmering violet silk.

Betsy flew straight into her arms. "Grandmother!"

"Welcome home, little granddaughter."

Mary stood waiting. She caught a glimpse of open doors in the hall beyond. There were graceful chairs and tables. There were oil portraits in dull-gold frames. There were delicate ornaments and gleaming crystal here and there.

The white-haired lady turned to Mary. She placed an arm around her and smiled. "So this is my other granddaughter."

Mary liked her at once. There was something warm and nice about her welcome. Mary felt as though she were blood-kin. Of course she really wasn't. Grandmother Humphreys was Ma's mother, and Ma was only Mary's step-mother.

Grandmother Humphreys led the way into a cool room where the shades were drawn to keep out the summer sun. It was pleasant after the long hot drive from Lexington.

"I'll ring for Jane. You girls must be tired and thirsty," Grandmother Humphreys said.

Mary settled down into the depths of a large chair and looked around the room. At the first glance she saw her face reflected in the long mirror on the opposite wall. Then she noticed the bookcase filled with leather-bound books. Nearby were crossed swords over a portrait of a Revolutionary officer in buff and blue. It was a room filled with interesting things.

In a short time a pleasant-looking young Negro woman carrying a large silver tray entered the room. She set the tray beside Mrs. Humphreys.

"Thank you, Jane. I'm sure my granddaughters will enjoy the refreshment," Grandmother Humphreys said.

"Do you have a new granddaughter, ma'am?" Jane asked, smiling at Mary.

"Indeed I do. She's Mary Todd, and she comes from Lexington."

Jane's smile widened. "It'll be nice to have young faces in the house again."

"Well, I hope you have liked my face," Grandmother Humphreys said tartly.

Jane looked confused for a minute. Then she saw the twinkle in the old lady's eyes. "Oh, yes, ma'am. Yes, indeed, ma'am!"

She was chuckling softly to herself as she went out. Mary sat watching the scene with interest. Now she turned to Grandmother and spoke in a puzzled way. "I don't understand. At home we're kind to our slaves. We're fond of them. Mammy Sally is terribly bossy, but I love her anyway. But you treated Jane more as a friend than as a slave."

"She is a friend," the old lady returned promptly. "Nobody ever had a better friend. She's kind, thoughtful, honest, and intelligent."

Mary looked puzzled. "But she is still a slave."

"By the mistaken laws of the land, she is. But she and the other Negroes who live on my place will be freed after my death."

"E-man-ci-pa-ted," Mary said.

Grandmother Humphreys smiled. "A big word for such a little girl."

"I hear Pa and his visitors discussing it all the time," Mary told her.

Grandmother Humphreys looked serious. "Slavery is too big a question for any of us to settle easily. We've had it a long time. Many of us wish the slaves could be freed tomorrow. But they've grown used to having their masters take care of them. Could they take care of themselves right away? Most of them, you know, can neither read nor write."

"Is that their fault?" Mary asked.

"Of course not, but it's true."

"They want to be free, don't they?" Mary persisted.

"Some do and some don't," Grandmother Humphreys answered. "Many of them—like Jane—feel they're actually a part of the family

106

to whom they belong. Well, maybe time will settle the slavery question."

"But I've heard visitors at our house say the North won't give us time. A lot of people up there want slavery stopped quick."

"Oh, yes," said Grandmother Humphreys, "but they're wrong, too. If they had their way it would mean distress for the Negroes, as I've said. It would ruin many whites who have put their money in Negro labor."

"But that doesn't make slavery right, does it, Grandmother?" Betsy wanted to know.

"Of course it doesn't, child. Many of us Southerners who own slaves know it, but we don't know what to do about it. We just try to do what is best for our slaves, and we try to do what is best for the country."

"What is best for the country?" Mary said.

Grandmother smiled. "What questions you ask an old lady! It takes a wiser head than mine to answer them. But I know that we should try always to keep a united country. Then, given time, maybe we can work out this slavery problem. Meanwhile, I guess we're like the man who had the bull by the tail and couldn't let go."

Mary and Betsy laughed heartily. The idea of Grandmother Humphreys, who was like a fragile bit of Dresden china, holding a bull by the tail was too much for them. She smiled at their glee.

By now they had finished their tall frosted glasses of chilled grape juice. Jane came in to carry away the tray and glasses. Again Mary had the feeling that Grandmother Humphreys treated her more like a friend than a servant. This place was different.

Mary's busy eyes began to dart here and there. She thought the house was fascinating.

The old lady noticed her interest. "Would you like to hear about some of the things you're seeing?" she asked Mary. "Betsy has seen them all many times, but I don't think she will mind if I show them to you."

"I love to hear you tell about them," Betsy said quickly.

The two girls trailed around after the old lady. Mary watched Grandmother's thin, blue-veined hands linger lovingly on each object as she spoke of it.

"Much of the furniture came in over the Wilderness Road, which was first blazed by Daniel Boone," she said. "Frankfort had only a few hundred people when I came here to live near my brothers. I was a widow. My husband had died back in Virginia."

She paused before the portrait of a strong-faced, kind-eyed gentleman in early middle age. "This is his portrait," she said softly. "He was well-known and well-loved. He left me the greatest heritage a man can leave—the memory of a good life usefully lived. You, too, will aways be proud of your Grandfather Humphreys."

The girls were silent for a few minutes. Then Mary spoke again. "You have so many lovely things, Grandmother Humphreys."

"I suppose I do," the old lady agreed. "My brother James was once the minister to France. He brought me many souvenirs of his stay in that country." Her eyes rested on a rare vase.

Betsy was studying the portraits. "Just think, Mary, someday you and I will marry men like these. Their portraits will hang on the walls of our homes, and we'll show them to our grandchildren."

Mary frowned. She seemed uncertain how to put her thoughts into words. Then her firm chin went out at a stubborn angle. "I don't know what sort of man I shall marry, but I am certain that I'd rather marry a good man than the richest man in the world."

110

"Bravo!" Grandmother Humphreys tapped her fingers together softly. She looked at Mary with affection. "Hold fast to that idea, little granddaughter. Someday it should bring you the best of husbands."

Mary smiled. "And I'll see that other people know how good he is."

Later that night Mary and Betsy settled down between lavender-scented sheets in an upstairs bedroom with a sloping ceiling. Mary smiled happily. Then she spoke aloud. She seemed to be talking to herself more than to Betsy.

"When I'm grown-up, if I can be just like Grandmother Humphreys, I'll be perfectly satisfied with myself."

Invitation to a Ball

MARY and Betsy were at breakfast with Grandmother Humphreys. Jane had just brought in a great crystal bowl of huge red strawberries. She placed it in front of her mistress.

Grandmother picked up a big silver berry spoon. She ladled the berries into saucers. Jane handed the saucers to Mary and Betsy.

Mary sprinkled her berries with sugar. Then she poured thick cream over them from a fat pitcher. "Um-m-m!" she said, tasting them. "The best strawberries in the whole world must grow on your place, Grandmother."

Grandmother smiled. "I'm glad you like them."

The bell rope at the front door jingled. A moment later Grandmother's coachman John entered the room. He carried a large square envelope on a small silver tray. He handed it to Grandmother.

Mary watched eagerly. The old lady reached for her spectacles. She opened the envelope. Then she read the message. Mary and Betsy waited impatiently.

At last Grandmother looked up. There was a pleasant smile on her fine old features. "An invitation to a ball, my dears."

"A ball?" Mary repeated. There were balls in Lexington, but twelve-year-old girls like Mary and Betsy never went to them. It was fun to hear the older girls tell about them.

"I've been invited to a large ball next week," Grandmother explained. "Half of Frankfort will be there. Have you girls ever been to a big fashionable ball?"

113

They shook their heads. "No, Grandmother," Mary said.

"The note from my hostess says I may bring you if I care to. Would you like that?"

They could not believe their ears. Mary clapped her hands in delight. Betsy gave a gasp of surprise.

Luckily they could not read her mind. "I'm afraid they will sit back against the wall like a couple of little sticks," she was thinking. "Still they might have a good time looking on. They will talk about it for weeks."

She rose briskly from the breakfast table. "We must be thinking of what we will wear," she told the girls.

At last the night came. Mary and Betsy were dressed by eight o'clock. Grandmother Humphreys in her maroon-colored silk rustled down the hall to look them over.

Mary looked at the handsome old lady. Her

face was framed in a becoming cap of rare lace. The girl threw her arms about her. "Grandmother, you're beautiful!"

The old lady returned Mary's embrace. "And I shall be taking the loveliest girls in Frankfort to the ball with me."

An hour later the Humphreys' carriage rolled up to the door of a large red-brick mansion. Lights shone from every window. John climbed down from the coachman's box to open the door of the carriage for Grandmother and the girls.

Grandmother Humphreys went up the walk toward the wide front entrance. The girls followed her. Snatches of voices and laughter drifted out to them from the ballroom on the second floor. There were strains of music, too. Mary was so excited that she almost forgot to walk like a lady. She felt more like skipping.

As she reached the second floor of the house, Mary gasped with delight. She stepped through

the wide archway. To her it seemed an enchanted scene.

The ballroom extended all the way across the house. The crystal chandelier in the center of the ceiling was twice as large as the one in the Todd house. Long mirrors at either end of the room reflected the lights, the colors, and the gay company.

Mary drank in the sight of the ladies in their beautiful gowns and their escorts in evening dress. "All of Frankfort—not just half—must be here," she whispered to Grandmother.

Grandmother introduced Mary and Betsy to the host and hostess. Then she led the way to some chairs not far from the musicians. She motioned to the girls to sit down. "I'm too old and you're too young to take part in the dancing, but we will enjoy watching, won't we?"

For a while Mary and Betsy felt young and out of place. They sat back in their chairs against the wall, but their eyes were not still a minute.

Round and round the ballroom the couples went. Mary tried to look everywhere at once. At last the musicians struck up a waltz. The girls watched the dancers glide out onto the floor.

Mary noticed a handsome old gentleman with two tall boys. She guessed the boys were in their late teens. All three made their way toward Grandmother Humphreys and the two girls. They stopped in front of them.

The old gentleman made a courtly bow to Mrs. Humphreys. "What is this?" he asked, with a twinkle in his eyes. "The prettiest girl at the ball is not dancing."

Grandmother laughed merrily. "What nonsense you talk, James. Besides, I'm too old. My dancing days are over."

"They need not be," he said gallantly. "Will you lead the grand march with me, Sister?"

Grandmother's eyes shone with pleasure. "Indeed I will. We'll show these younger people how it should be done. But do you suppose you could find partners for my granddaughters, James?"

"I have them," he told her. "May I present Peyton Thompson and Joseph Lawrence? They're grandsons of a very good friend of mine."

A moment later Mary and Betsy found themselves out in the center of the smooth, polished floor. There was time only for Mary to give one happy glance at Betsy before she was whirled away. They were not too young after all!

By the time Peyton brought her back to her place, Mary was talking away at a great rate. Another young man was waiting to claim her. After that she and Betsy never lacked for partners.

It was long past midnight when the girls drove

away with Grandmother. Mary slipped her feet out of her satin slippers. "Oh, my feet hurt! But I've had a wonderful time."

Grandmother laughed. "Do you think you'll be satisfied to be a little girl again tomorrow?"

Mary nodded. "Tonight was perfect. I know Ma will never let me go to a ball at home until I'm older. I don't want to grow up yet, anyhow, but tonight I felt just like Cinderella."

Grandmother nodded approval. "Stay a little girl for a while longer, Mary. You will have your turn at being a princess one of these days."

Mary's Not a Bluestocking

"DON'T you think Dr. Ward is too strict when he expects his pupils to begin work at five in the morning?" Mrs. Todd asked her husband.

Mary looked up quickly from her French grammar. "Dr. Ward says our brains work better before our bodies are clogged with food. Besides, I don't mind five o'clock classes. We have a good breakfast at school at seven. After all, I'm not a child. I'm thirteen now."

"There is your answer," Mr. Todd told his wife.

Mary gathered up her papers from the table. "If you'll excuse me, I'll go upstairs and write

121

my French lesson for tomorrow. Dr. Ward has given us a very long assignment. I want to finish it before I go to bed."

After Mary had left the room, Mrs. Todd turned to her husband. "You don't suppose Mary is becoming a bluestocking when she is only thirteen, do you?"

Mr. Todd laughed at her fears. "Do you mean one of those too-educated persons who have no time to be womanly? Have you forgotten how she loves her dancing class? Or how she gave her good clothes away to poor little Tessie Gray, who lives out on the Frankfort turnpike? Or how she mothers every stray cat and dog for miles around? Or how she collects the younger children around her?"

"I suppose you're right," Mrs. Todd admitted.

Mr. Todd patted her on the shoulder. "Mary has an eager mind. She's thirsty for knowledge. As long as she keeps her interest in everything and everybody, and is kind, I'm not afraid of her becoming a bluestocking."

Early next morning Mary rose at dawn and dressed for school. She tiptoed down the stairs and out the front door so that she would not disturb the sleeping family.

As she hurried toward North Broadway, she could see the first pink streaks of sunrise in the sky. Only a few people were out on the streets. A spring wagon clattered past her. Mrs. Hostetter's son was driving it. He was taking a load of potatoes to the grocery store of Smith and Todd, where Mary's father was a partner. Mary waved to the Hostetter boy and hurried on.

She turned the corner and walked briskly up North Broadway. She remembered that the grandfather's clock on the stair landing at home had shown the time as a quarter to five.

"Oh, my!" Mary wailed to herself. "I must hurry. Dr. Ward rapped Ned Dunn on the back

123

of the hand with a ruler when he was late. I
don't believe he'd punish a girl that way, but I
don't want to chance it."

As Mary drew near Second Street, she heard
footsteps behind her. She glanced around. A big
policeman was hurrying along behind her.

"He must be the new one straight from Ireland that Pa told us about last night," she said to herself.

She crossed the street and started down Second Street. Again she looked over her shoulder. The policeman, too, had crossed. It looked almost as though he were following her.

Now she was opposite the big white house on the corner. The policeman seemed to be gaining on her. She frowned. She did not care to be pursued by a policeman.

"Hey, there!" he shouted.

Mary's scowl grew deeper. One block more and she'd be at the Academy. Its tall gray outlines rose before her in the early morning light.

"Stop, young lady!"

Mary tossed her head. She'd not be late just to satisfy a policeman's curiosity. Certainly she had nothing to discuss with him.

She picked up her skirts and looked about her.

No one except the policeman was in sight. No one would see her do such an unladylike thing as run. Her trim little feet fairly flew over the ground.

At the Academy she slipped through the big front door, hurried down the long hall, and walked into the classroom where the other boys and girls were already seated. Dr. Ward was in a back room drinking his morning cup of coffee.

The clock in the hall struck five times. As the last stroke sounded, the tall Episcopalian rector walked into the classroom. He was straight as an arrow. He looked to see whether everyone was present.

Mary was still panting. She rolled her eyes at her cousin Margaret Stuart. "I've had such a time!" she whispered.

"Miss Todd!" Dr. Ward's stern eyes were on her. "We will have no whispering, Miss Todd. Class will come to order."

Just then there was loud knocking at the front door. Dr. Ward strode out to answer it.

A moment later he returned to the classroom. Close behind him was the young policeman who had followed Mary. Her face turned scarlet.

"There she is!" the officer exclaimed. He pointed straight at Mary. All eyes were turned on her.

"You mean Mary Todd?" the rector exclaimed. "My best pupil? My prize French scholar? What in the world do you imagine she has done?"

The young Irishman was twisting his policeman's hat about in his hands. He stood first on one foot and then on the other.

"Perhaps I made a mistake, sir," he admitted. "But she hurried so fast—she refused to stop when I called to her——"

"And what if she did?" Dr. Ward demanded. "She was eager to be on time for her early class."

127

"Now I know, sir. It's all a big mistake—and I'd like to beg the young lady's pardon—but she had a parcel under her arm——"

"My best dress for Amy's party this afternoon," Mary said indignantly.

"I really thought——" the policeman began again.

"What did you think?" Dr. Ward sternly demanded of the young policeman.

"I figured she was on her way to meet some young man—an elopement——"

A howl of glee went up from the other pupils. For a moment Mary's eyes snapped. Then she, too, joined in the laughter.

Dr. Ward held up a hand for silence. The class became quiet at once, but the pupils were shaking with silent laughter.

There was amusement in Dr. Ward's voice. "You were certainly mistaken, officer, but no offense is taken. Just forget the whole matter."

The policeman backed out of the room. He was still apologizing.

The corners of Dr. Ward's grave mouth twitched in a slight smile. Then he became serious once more. "You may translate, Miss Mary."

Mary began to read the French exercise. With difficulty she controlled her voice. Her blue eyes were dancing. If her stepmother could have seen her now, she would have known that Mary would never be a bluestocking.

A Wedding in the Family

It was a few days before Christmas. Dr. Ward's Academy was dismissed for the holidays. Betsy Humphreys had already gone home to Frankfort.

Mary and her sister Elizabeth were cleaning the crystal chandelier that hung in the drawing room. That was their special job. No one else was trusted with the beautiful French fixture. The girls always handled the gleaming crystal prisms with the greatest care.

Mary was entertaining Elizabeth with the story of the policeman who had chased her all the way to school only the week before. Elizabeth had just returned yesterday from a visit in

the country. This was the first time she had heard about Mary's caper.

High up on the stepladder Mary handed down a prism to Elizabeth. She in turn wiped it with a damp cloth and handed it back to Mary. Sometimes it seemed to them both that there must be thousands of little glass pieces.

Today the time was passing fast. The memory of the policeman was still fresh in Mary's mind.

"And he thought I was eloping. Imagine! I know I'm tall for my age, but can you imagine me a bride? Or yourself? I suppose we'll marry someday, but that time seems a hundred years away."

Elizabeth threw her a quick glance. Mary was fastening a prism to the chandelier. She took off another gleaming bit of glass and handed it down to her sister.

"Time passes quickly sometimes, though," Mary continued. "Christmas is just around the corner. This is the last time we'll ever clean the chandelier. It makes me sad to think about it. We'll be in the red-brick house on Main Street by May. I'm glad Pa bought it. Do you remember the time I fell in the creek behind it?"

Elizabeth's eyes grew misty as she looked up at the girl on the ladder. She remembered well the saucy youngster on that long-ago day whose spirits the cold water could not chill.

"What makes you look so cowlike all of a sudden?" Mary teased her.

Elizabeth smiled mysteriously. "Wouldn't you like to know?"

Mary's mind was still on the Main Street house. "The flowers will be beautiful then. The roses will be out and the lilacs——"

"I'm afraid I won't be there to see them."

Mary stared down at her. "What do you mean?"

Elizabeth smiled. "I didn't mean to break the news so soon. Eighteen hundred thirty-two will be a very special year for me, Mary. I'm going to marry Ninian Edwards in February—— Mary! Do be careful!"

The ladder swayed. Then it settled slowly into place. Mary scampered down and threw her arms about her sister. "You goose! Do you want to turn your wedding day into my funeral? Don't ever tell me such startling news when I'm perched on a ladder."

"Aren't you surprised?"

Mary held her at arm's length and considered. "Well, yes and no. How could I be when Ninian has been underfoot for two years? Shall you go to live in Illinois?"

Elizabeth nodded. "You know his father has been governor of Illinois twice. He may be again. Since Mrs. Edwards is dead, look where that places me, Mary. I may be hostess at the governor's mansion someday. I'm only sixteen. Do you suppose I shall be up to it?"

"If you aren't, Ma has wasted a lot of time and energy on you," Mary answered. "Anyone who can satisfy Ma would shine in the capital of the United States—not to mention the capital of Illinois. Oh, Elizabeth—a wedding in our family!"

Christmas came and went. The days flew by. The wedding day came closer. Elizabeth had decided on a quiet wedding with only a few friends and relatives as guests.

At last the February day dawned cold and clear. There was a light dry snow on the ground. That afternoon the guests' feet crunched through it as they came up the steps from the street. All the Todd relatives were there. Grandmother Parker came, too.

Mary was in her glory. For the occasion Ma had allowed her to catch up her hair in a bunch of curls on her neck. She wore a blue velvet frock that reflected the blue of her eyes. Since Frances was to be her sister's only bridesmaid, Mary was free to welcome the guests.

As she hurried from one group to another, she almost ran into a tall, broad-shouldered youth with coal-black hair and dark glowing eyes. "Why, Cassius Clay!" she exclaimed. "You've

gone up north and changed so that for a moment I hardly knew you."

The twenty-two-year-old cousin of Mr. Henry Clay grinned from ear to ear. "And you must be little Mary Todd. You've changed, too. The last time I saw you, you were bouncing up and down on Snowball."

"Well, I don't bounce now," Mary answered with a grin. "And if you're looking for Mary Jane Warfield every time you roll your eyes about, you're wasting your time. She's late, as usual."

Cassius Clay smiled broadly. "Pepper-pot!"

"Sh-h!"

From a corner of the drawing room came the music of the wedding march. The Reverend Robert Stuart walked out from the library. Ninian Edwards and his father came from the morning room. Frances in pink taffeta rustled through the archway.

Mary's eyes turned upward as Elizabeth, in her mother's white satin wedding dress, descended the broad stairs. In her hand she carried a white prayer book.

It was a simple service. The afternoon sunlight made a shaft of gold through the front windows. Mary, looking on, remembered what she'd said before Christmas. She hoped her wedding day was not, after all, a hundred years off.

The young couple left while the reception was in full sway. At the door Mary clung to her oldest sister. It was hard to realize that she was going away for good. She and Ninian had found a small house where they would live until he graduated from Transylvania College.

"I hate to see you go even though we have fussed and scrapped a lot," Mary whispered to Elizabeth.

Elizabeth gave her a little squeeze. "We won't do it any more," she told Mary.

"Oh, yes, we will!" Mary laughed. "We're both Todds. All Todds fuss with one another and everyone else—especially with one another."

Elizabeth laughed, too. "Maybe you're right, Mary. Anyway, you shall come to live with me in Illinois someday. Temper and all, you're the best company I know of. And I love you."

The Taming
of a Wildcat

"MARY, come down off that roof! At once!"
Mary was perched on the ridgepole of the
carriage house. She looked down at her mother.

There was anxiety in every note of Mrs. Todd's
voice. She looked fearfully upward.

Mary arose. She balanced a foot on each side
of the roof. She shaded her eyes with one hand
and looked across the Catholic churchyard toward North Broadway. "The view from up here
is wonderful, Ma."

"Mary! Come down from there this minute!"

"Do you really mean it, Ma?" There was mischief in Mary's tone.

"Certainly I mean it," Mrs. Todd said grimly.

Whoosh! Mary suddenly disappeared from view. Mrs. Todd turned pale. She rushed to the far side of the carriage house.

Mary was climbing from a huge pile of leaves which Nelson had raked into a heap. She was rubbing her lip gingerly. "Ouch! That hurt," she exclaimed. "I bit it when I landed."

"I thought you had broken your neck," Mrs. Todd moaned. "Oh, Mary, you nearly frightened me to death!"

"Now, Ma, you know you always said I was born to get into trouble," Mary said kindly. "Besides, that roof isn't very high. I've jumped off it lots of times."

"You're going on fourteen," Mrs. Todd said indignantly. "It's high time you were growing up."

She stalked away and disappeared into the house. Mary looked thoughtfully after her.

"Maybe she's right," she said to herself. "Perhaps I'd better do as Reverend Wilson is always advising. Maybe I'd better cast off childish ways."

Before supper that night Mary went into her father's study. She half expected a scolding. She sat down beside him on the sofa and edged within the circle of his arm. "I've been a bad girl, Pa," she began.

"Yes, I heard," Robert Todd said.

Mary sighed. "Ma has already told you?"

He nodded. A slight smile played about his mouth. "You frightened her."

Mary's keen eyes caught the smile. "Then you aren't angry with me? I'm so glad."

Mr. Todd puffed on his cigar. "What happened helped me to make up my mind about something."

"Tell me," Mary said eagerly.

Her father shook his head. "Never mind now.

I'll tell you at supper. I think the whole family will be interested in my news."

Mary's eyes danced. "Then it isn't a punishment?"

He shook his head and smiled. "I don't regard it as one. I hope you won't."

The evening meal was unusually happy. Since Frances had gone to live with Elizabeth in Illinois, Mary was the eldest daughter of the house. She led the other boys and girls in lively chatter throughout the main course.

After Chaney had brought in the dessert and departed, Mr. Todd looked around the table. "I have a surprise for you, especially for Mary."

Mary beamed. Now she would find out.

Her father continued. "Before long Mary will be a young lady. Ma and I have decided to send her to a finishing school. After Christmas she will enroll at Madame Mentelle's boarding school on the Richmond Pike."

Mary could hardly believe her ears. All her life she had dreamed of going to a boarding school. And now——

"Madame Mentelle is a very great lady, in my opinion," Mr. Todd went on. Then suddenly he asked, "What do you know about the French Revolution, Levi?"

"Well, I—er——" Levi hesitated.

"I know all about it," Mary said promptly. She threw back her head and began to recite what she had learned from her history book: "The poor folk in France rose up against their rulers. They stormed the prison known as the Bastille and set the prisoners free. Then they seized King Louis XVI and his queen, Marie Antoinette——"

"That's enough," her father interrupted. "I see you know your history. I suppose you know, too, that there followed the time called the Reign of Terror. Those were unhappy days for France.

No persons who had ever been friendly toward the king and queen were safe."

"Had Madame Mentelle been friendly with them?" Mary asked.

Mr. Todd nodded. "In a way, yes. She and her husband were a part of the French court. Somehow they managed to escape. They crossed the Atlantic Ocean and came to the United States. At last they made their way to Lexington. For many years they've been good American citizens here."

Mary's face was wreathed in smiles. "And I'm going to her wonderful boarding school! I've heard the older girls talk about it for a long time."

The other children looked at Mary as though a fairy godmother had suddenly touched her with a magic wand.

"You'll get to stay there from Monday until Friday," Ann Maria told her enviously.

"They say Madame Mentelle won't allow her pupils to speak anything but French. Maybe you'll forget how to speak English," Levi offered.

Margaret and George set up a howl. "Who'll read to us?"—— "Who'll tell us stories?"—— "Nobody tells stories as well as you do." The questions came thick and fast.

Mary reached over and dropped a kiss on George's head. "I'll save my stories for weekends."

She looked at Betsy. Then she looked past her at her father. "What about Betsy? Won't she go with me?"

"Betsy still has work to finish at Dr. Ward's. She'll enroll at the Mentelle school later."

Betsy made no reply, but her eyes shone.

That night Mary sat up in bed. The pillows were piled high behind her head. Her blue eyes shone. Her voice rang with happiness. "I can't believe I'm really going. I've wanted to go to Madame Mentelle's ever since I can remember."

"And I'll be there, too, before long," Betsy said joyfully.

Mary gave her a cousinly pat. She went on talking. "Madame Victorie Charlotte Leclerc Mentelle," she whispered to herself. "Doesn't that sound romantic? Just think! She and her husband really lived in France during the days of the guillotine."

"The guillotine? What's that?" Betsy asked.

"It was a sort of big knife," Mary told her. "If you were an enemy of the people, *snip!* went your head. Heads were chopped off like so many cabbages. If the Mentelles had not fled the country, their heads would have rolled, too."

The girls lay for several minutes without speaking. In their peaceful Kentucky town it was difficult for them to imagine the scenes of the French Revolution. Mary broke the silence.

148

"I love to watch Madame Mentelle ride down the street in her carriage. She sits so straight and proud. Queen Marie Antoinette must have looked like her when she rode in a cart to the guillotine."

"Well, Madame Mentelle doesn't have to worry about losing her head," practical Betsy commented.

Mary giggled. "No, I suppose not. Madame Mentelle's probably planning how to make ladies out of wildcats like me. You know what Ma always says, 'It takes seven generations to make a lady.' The Todds have been at it for a long time. We can trace back lots farther than seven generations. It must take longer than that because Mammy Sally still reminds me to be a lady. I'm afraid Madame Mentelle has a big job before her."

Betsy smiled gleefully. "And she'll soon have to start on me. Poor lady!"

Mary's eyes danced. "What fun we'll have when you enroll there, too! Oh, Betsy, do study hard so you can come soon!"

"I will," Betsy promised.

Mary's eyes glowed at the thought of the months ahead. "I can hardly wait until after Christmas. I wonder if it's true about speaking French. I know the pupils have to speak it at meals." Her eyes widened. "Betsy, what if I don't learn French fast enough? Do you suppose I shall starve to death?"

The Glass Slipper

"Don't you think things are getting a little dull here?" Mary asked.

"Not when you're around," Susan Warfield giggled. "Somehow you manage to keep a place rather lively."

Some of the students at Madame Mentelle's were gathered on the long low front porch of the school. Classes were over for the day. The girls were waiting in the twilight for supper to be announced.

"I'll never forget the trick you played on Sallie Turner," Amelia Carter told Mary. "She really thought you were a French friend of Madame

Mentelle's that day you walked into the music room."

Mary smiled impishly. "That was easy. She couldn't possibly have recognized me beneath the veil I was wearing. You must admit my French accent isn't too bad. *Bon jour, ma chère petite fille*—good morning, my dear little girl. Where is my friend, Madame Mentelle?"

The girls laughed admiringly. "And Sallie made you a very respectful bow," Josephine Parker recalled. "Then she told you that Madame was out for a drive. She even went to get you a glass of lemonade."

"That lemonade was too much for me," Mary admitted. "Though maybe I wouldn't have choked on it if I hadn't been trying so hard not to laugh."

"Whatever made you think of the idea in the first place?" Susan asked.

Mary raised her eyebrows. "Don't you know?

152

It was one way to stop Sallie from practicing scales. She had run up and down the keyboard for hours."

A burst of laughter greeted Mary's admission. "What are you going to do next, Mary?" Amelia demanded.

"I haven't quite decided," Mary said. She looked off across the lawn for a moment. "Don't you think a play would be fun? A play with lots of action and pretty costumes?"

"Oh, yes," Amelia agreed. "That sounds wonderful."

"When do we start?" another girl asked.

"*Where* do we start?" Mary asked thoughtfully. She looked from one to the other. "Of course, there's the carriage house, but Madame's coachman guards it as though he were a dragon. We simply must have a stage—but where?"

"Why don't you leave that to me?" a soft voice behind them inquired.

The girls turned quickly. Madame Mentelle was standing in the doorway. With her white hair piled high on her head she had a queenly look. In the dusk Mary could almost imagine a crown on her head.

"Won't you sit down?" Mary invited. She hastened to offer Madame her chair.

Madame sat down in the midst of the little group. She smiled into their eager faces. "So you are planning a play."

"May we, Madame?"

"Would it be possible?"

"Will you let us spare the time from lessons?"

Madame raised a hand. "Please, one at a time, my dears. Yes, I think it could be arranged. What do you have in mind?"

Mary spoke first. "Could it be something French, Madame?"

Madame smiled at Mary. "That sounds very nice to me. But what will you do for men in this play? Even a play world on the stage would be a poor place without them, and our school is only for young ladies."

Mary's eyes suddenly lighted up. "I know what we could do. Let's have a play about Cinderella. I was reading the story to my little sister only last week. Girls could take men's parts in that story. They wouldn't look at all silly in those beautiful French court costumes."

"Excellent!" Madame exclaimed. She seemed as interested as the girls.

"I can see it now," Mary told the group. "The magic pumpkin coach—the ugly stepmother and sisters—poor little Cinderella among the ashes and later a beautiful princess at the ball. Oh, Madame, can't you just see those dancing couples and hear the violins?"

Madame smiled at the girls. "I think Mary will write your play—in French."

A delighted chorus of voices greeted her announcement. Only Mary was speechless. Finally she recovered her voice. "In French?"

"Yes," Madame said briskly. "Who could do it better? Come to my sitting room after study hall, Mary, and we'll talk it over. Supper is ready, girls. Shall we go in?" As quickly as that, Mary was given the new task.

For the next few weeks Mary spent many hours curled up in the low crotch of the old apple tree behind the school. This was her favorite spot since she had begun to put *Cinderella* into play form. This afternoon with a book of French fairy tales and a French grammar close at hand she was scratching busily away on a pad of white paper.

She did not hear Madame Mentelle coming across the lawn. Not until Madame spoke did Mary come out of a make-believe world back to the present.

She hastily scrambled down from the tree.

"I'm sorry you caught me in such an undigni-
fied position, but it's such a good place to write."

Madame laid a hand on the trunk of the tree.
Her eyes had a faraway look. "It reminds me of
a tree long ago in France, and you remind me
of a sixteen-year-old girl—who was I."

Mary's cheeks were pink with pleasure. "Oh, Madame, that's the nicest thing you could say to me! But how could I seem like you? You're always a lady. You never talk too loud. You never lose your temper."

Madame sat down on the bench under the tree and drew Mary down beside her. "I've been trying longer than you have. How is the play going?"

Mary frowned. "I don't know. Sometimes I can hardly write fast enough to get my thoughts down. Then again I can't think of a single word."

"Suppose you read it to me," Madame suggested.

She listened carefully. Mary's musical young voice was the only sound in the garden except the twittering of birds and the rustling of leaves. Once in a while the girl stumbled over a French word. Then Madame repeated it for her.

When Mary finished, she laid down the play and looked up. Madame nodded approvingly. "A fine piece of work. I'm very proud of you."

"Thank you, Madame," Mary answered. "I wish I could have done it better. I know what I want to say, but I can't find the right words."

"I see that you found one somebody missed a long time ago." Madame's eyes twinkled. "Cinderella really wore a slipper of fur—*vair*—instead of glass, or *verre*."

Mary's face lighted up. "I didn't know it was really fur until I read the French version."

Madame smiled. "Someone wasn't too careful when he translated it into English years ago. But our audience will expect a glass slipper, so perhaps we had better say it is glass."

"All right," Mary agreed. "That's a small matter. But I still wish I could have written a better play."

Madame patted her hand. "If we're the right

159

sort of people, we're never quite satisfied with our efforts, my dear. Our lives are like the glorious cathedrals in France. Their tall spires soar upward like fingers pointing to heaven. They seem to be reaching out for what they will never attain. We human beings, too, may do our best, but we can never quite attain our goals."

"I don't even know what my goal is," Mary confessed. "There's so much I want to do and so much I want to learn, Madame. Why can't girls go to college as boys do?"

"They will someday," Madame told her. "In the meantime, with your mind you will keep learning all your life. You possess something even better than a good mind. You have a gift for living, Mary, which is given to few people. *Joie de vivre* they call it in my native tongue. It means joy of living."

Mary drew a deep sigh. "You make me feel so happy, Madame. These years in your school have been wonderful. I'll never forget them as long as I live."

The night of the play was a perfect June night. In the spacious garden of the school, workmen had built a high, wide backdrop for the play *Cinderella*.

About two hundred people were in the audience. There were proud fathers and mothers. There were noisy, squirming little brothers and sisters. There were adoring uncles and aunts. Nearly all the patrons of the school had gathered to see *Cinderella*.

Presently Madame Mentelle appeared in front of the curtains. A ripple of admiration ran through the crowd. Not a sound was heard as she began to speak.

"My friends, it gives me great pleasure to welcome you to our play which marks the end of the school year. I am happy to tell you that every word of it will be spoken in French. Furthermore, it was written by one of the school's own pupils—Mary Todd."

Down in the audience Robert Todd and his wife exchanged happy glances. There was no time for comments. The curtains were parting.

The young Todds sat as though they were under a spell. So did all the other children in the audience. Before their eyes the pictures of one of their favorite fairy tales came to life.

There was the familiar scene of poor Cinderella in her rags watching her stepmother and stepsisters get ready for the ball. Josephine Parker and the girls who played the sisters outdid themselves in haughty bad manners. Then they swept off the stage and left the heroine alone.

But presto!—the godmother with her magic wand arrived. Close on her heels came a yellow pumpkin-shaped coach drawn by six oversized gray mice. The coach seemed rather wobbly. From the amusement that rippled through the

crowd, the onlookers were guessing which girls acted as mice. At the end of the act Cinderella departed joyfully for the ball.

After a short interval the curtains opened again. A gasp of pleasure went up from the audience. It was a beautiful scene. Against the backdrop rose a pink-and-silver throne. In front of the throne couples danced gracefully in a fairy-tale ballroom—the lawn. When Cinderella arrived, she at once became the belle of the ball. Finally twelve ringing notes—to show midnight—sounded behind the backdrop. Cinderella ran swiftly off the stage.

During the second intermission friends from all sides came to speak to Mr. and Mrs. Todd. Mr. Henry Clay was one. "I always knew Mary would make her mark!" he exclaimed. "Even when she was a little thing, she liked to speak French."

The last act was short. The scene was the same

164

as the first. The prince's messenger came in with the glass slipper on a pillow. After useless attempts on the part of the stepsisters to force the slipper on their feet, Cinderella drew it on easily. The prince—Susan Warfield made a handsome prince—arrived to claim her as his bride. The play ended.

The curtains closed with lively applause. The actors took a curtain call. Then someone shouted, "Author! Author!"

Soon Mary appeared on the stage. In her arms was a large bouquet of roses which Madame had given her. Her face was wreathed in smiles. She bowed gracefully toward the audience.

"Speech!" someone called.

Mary gasped. Then she found her voice and spoke clearly. "I really don't deserve this," she told them simply. "I made a little play from an old familiar story. That's all. But thank you— thank you, anyway."

Robert Todd and his wife were waiting for her when she came from backstage. Mary caught sight of them as soon as she entered the garden. She walked straight to them and slipped a hand into her father's. "Pa!" she said.

He held her at arm's length. "I'm proud of you."

Ma slipped a hand into Mary's other one. "You're really a grown young lady, Mary. Our tomboy seems gone forever."

Mary smiled. "Oh, I don't know. Perhaps I could bring her back." She shook her head. "No, I don't believe I could, and I don't want to. I guess I've grown up for keeps. And thanks, both of you, for everything."

A Trip to
Springfield

THERE was an unusual bustle in the long red-brick passenger station of the Lexington and Ohio Railroad at Mill and Water streets. The Todds had come to see Mary off on a visit to Springfield, Illinois. They made a large number since she had two brothers and a sister still living at home, not to mention four half brothers and half sisters. The oldest sister Elizabeth and her husband Ninian now lived in Springfield.

"Now, Mary, promise me you won't talk with strangers," her mother said. "An eighteen-year-old girl has to be careful."

"Ma, you know I can't promise that," Mary

167

protested. "I simply must talk with someone——"

"Or bust," seven-year-old Sam finished for her.

"Burst, Sam," Mary corrected him. "However,
I promise not to talk with any young men. Will
that do, Ma?"

Mrs. Todd sighed. "I suppose it will have to."

"I wish I were going with you," ten-year-old
George told her. "Lucky you! Those cars whiz
along at twenty-five miles an hour."

"I remember when Mr. Clay took me to see a
tiny model railroad," Mary told her family. "He
said then there would someday be a real one between Lexington and Frankfort, but I'm sure
he didn't know how fast the cars would travel."

Mrs. Todd turned to her husband. "I almost
wish we hadn't promised Mary this visit to her
sisters. Do you feel that it's safe, Robert?"

"There, there!" he told his wife. "We must
keep up with the times, my dear. The railroad

is as safe as any other means of transportation. Even horses run away."

Mrs. Todd looked doubtful. "I'd feel so much better if she were going in the carriage with Old Nelson than on this—this monster." She pointed to the little steam locomotive puffing away on the track.

A thought suddenly occurred to her. "Mary, perhaps you should get out at the top of the Frankfort hill and ride down in the stagecoach."

"Ma! There hasn't been an accident since the coach flew off the tracks five years ago," Levi protested.

Mary bit the cross words that rose to her lips. Ma was about to take half the joy out of the trip.

"Daughter, come over here. I must give you your tickets and your money." Mr. Todd drew Mary aside. "Don't worry about what your mother said, my dear. She's always a little nervous. You may stay on the train and ride down into Frankfort if you like. There seems to be very little danger since the steamcars have been improved."

"Pa, you're so good to me." Mary looked up into her father's kind face.

She wished for a moment that she were not leaving Lexington for the summer. Somehow she felt she was leaving her childhood behind. Of course, she had really already done that several years ago. But this change seemed so definite. Things would never be quite the same again.

"All a-bo-a-ard!" The conductor leaned from the rear of the single coach behind the locomotive. The engine began to get up steam— *puff-puff-puff*.

A thin line of passengers trickled out the station door. There were eleven in all. Two were farmers traveling out to the country. There was a woman with a small boy and a crying baby.

170

There was Mrs. Hinton, a friend of the family in whose care Mary would travel as far as Louisville. The other passengers were gentlemen of various ages. "No young ones," Mary noted. "That should satisfy Ma."

"Here!" Mary's small half brother Sam thrust a covered basket into her hands.

"What's this, Sam?"

"My very best garter snake. I know how you like pets. I'm going to let you take him all the way to Springfield."

Mary stared with horror at the basket in her hands. She hastily hid her feelings. She stooped and kissed her little brother on the top of his tousled head. "Thank you, darling. I'm going to miss you." She held the basket before her safely at an arm's length.

"Come, Mary." Her father led her across the platform toward the train. Before she had time to realize she was leaving, she found herself in-

side the coach and seated by an open window. She waved good-by to the Todds on the platform. The wheels had begun to turn.

"Give me that basket!"

Levi stood beside her. He was grinning broadly. Mary was thankful to hand it over. The passengers smiled at the sight of the tall young fellow with the covered basket, running down the aisle. Only he and Mary knew what was in it.

"Don't let Sam find out," Mary called after him.

"I won't," he promised.

Now the train was rolling faster. A passenger across the aisle thrust his head out the window. "He made it," he announced to Mary.

With a sigh Mary settled back in her seat. Levi had come to her rescue. He was a good brother even if he had teased her a lot when both of them were younger.

She looked back. Her family waved at her. She blew them a kiss. Then she drew in her arm.

She would miss them, but a whole summer in Springfield lay ahead—Elizabeth and Frances, their husbands, new friends, gay parties. Who could say what else? Maybe a whole new life. Well, let it come. She was ready for it.

Mary had a wonderful visit in Springfield. She had many relatives there besides her two married sisters, Elizabeth Edwards and Frances Wallace. There was her uncle, John Todd, with two daughters about Mary's age. There was her cousin and childhood playmate, John Todd Stuart. He now had a wife and a family of growing children.

One day he said to her, "Mary, I'd like to have you meet my law partner, Abraham Lincoln."

"Where is he?" Mary asked. "Everywhere I go I hear his name mentioned."

"He's away from Springfield at present," John

told her. "He's at Vandalia. Some people want to keep the state capital there. Lincoln wants it here. It will be here—he's a fighter. He doesn't give up when he thinks he's right."

"I like that. I'm a fighter, too!" Mary answered with a twinkle in her eyes.

John laughed. He knew it to be true.

"Is he handsome?" Mary asked.

"Well, not exactly." John read the disappointment in his cousin's eyes. "But he's the smartest man I've ever met. He knows law from A to Z. He remembers everything he reads. He loves poetry almost as much as you love it. He simply couldn't do a dishonest or a wrong thing. And he tells the best jokes I've ever heard."

"He sounds interesting," Mary said.

She did not meet her cousin's law partner on this trip. He did not return to Springfield before she went back to Lexington.

Mrs. Abraham Lincoln

Two years later, in 1839, Mary returned to Springfield to stay. This time she met young Abraham Lincoln. He stood six feet four inches tall. He towered above her. She had never seen such kindness in any face. They were attracted to each other at once.

On November 4, 1842, Mary Todd and Abraham Lincoln were married.

Mary had been born in a bluegrass home of culture and refinement. Abe had been born in a log cabin on the Kentucky frontier. Their first home together was a room in a Springfield boardinghouse called the Globe Tavern.

176

Young Mrs. Lincoln loved the bustle and excitement of the tavern. Whenever the big bell on the roof rang to announce the arrival of a stagecoach, she would hurry to the window to see the passengers alight.

She watched out of that same window every night for her tall, dark-haired husband who hurried home to her from his law office.

In these times lawyers had to be away from home a great deal. Since the people could not come to the courts because of the hardships of travel, the courts went to the people. Abraham Lincoln went with them. He was gone as much as three months at a time. Mary was lonely without him.

But she soon had company. In August, 1843, a little son was born to the Lincolns. "We'll name him Robert Todd Lincoln," Mary said. She was thinking of Pa, miles away in Lexington, Kentucky.

"This baby must have a real home," Abe said. "There's a house for sale on Eighth and Jackson streets. It's near my law office."

The Lincolns soon moved into the modest house. Soon after they moved, another baby arrived. They named him Edward Baker Lincoln and called him Eddie. Their family was growing. Now it was 1846.

In the fall of 1847, Mary Lincoln with her husband and her two sons began the long journey to her girlhood home in Kentucky. The trip by stagecoach from Springfield, Illinois, to Saint Louis, Missouri, was slow and tiresome. In Saint Louis they boarded a steamboat for the pleasant second lap of their trip.

Mary stood beside her tall husband as the boat pulled away from the shore. He had little Eddie in his arms. Bobbie was holding fast to his father's coattails. Mary's face was full of pride.

"How happy I shall be when we get to Lex-

ington," she declared. "Father is the only one in the family who has met you. Even he has never seen Eddie. I want to show my wonderful husband and children to the folks in my own home town."

Abraham shook his head. "The children do well enough, but your husband isn't much to show off. I'm not exactly handsome, Mary."

"Everyone says you look distinguished," Mary protested. "You are distinguished. Haven't the voters just made you a Congressman? They won't stop until they make you President."

Lincoln threw back his head and gave a hearty laugh. "That's a good joke!"

Mary's eyes flashed. "Wait and see."

After a week's journey the Lincolns arrived in Lexington. All the members of Mary's family were gathered at the Todd home to meet them.

There were her father and her stepmother. There were her own brothers, Levi and George, and her sister, Ann Maria. There were all Mr. Todd's children by his second marriage. The family servants were there in the background.

Mary's head swam at the sight of so many dear, familiar faces. She stepped forward. "I've brought the best husband and children in the world to the best folks any girl ever had."

Everyone everywhere liked the tall, lanky,

friendly, slow-spoken young man, with his dry wit and droll stories. Mary's family was no exception. They took him to their hearts.

Mary and the boys went on to Washington with her husband after the Lexington visit was ended. There they spent a happy winter together in the nation's capital. But a boarding-house proved a poor place for lively little boys.

In the spring of 1848 Mary took the youngsters back to Springfield. Mr. Lincoln came home as soon as he could leave his duties in Washington.

One day he had an important letter. President Fillmore offered him the governorship of Oregon Territory. Abraham Lincoln was overjoyed. He waved the letter in the air.

"Hurrah!" he shouted. He reached down and picked up Robert. He tossed him up in the air. Robert shrieked with delight. Mary stood by without a word. Her husband gave her a big bear hug. "You'll be the governor's lady, Mary," he told her.

She shook her head. Abraham's face fell. He had thought she would be happy.

"No," she said firmly. "We do not want to go to the Far West to rear our children. Some day it will be a great country, but now it hasn't the best schools. Besides you were made for bigger things. 'Way out there, you'd be forgotten. No one would think of you. I'm sure I'm right. Let's stay here."

He smiled that patient smile of his. "I trust your judgment about the children, Mary."

The Lincolns stayed in Springfield.

In 1850 the Lincolns were saddened by the death of little Eddie, who was then nearly four years old. At first Mary did not feel like going on. Nevertheless, knowing she must think about her husband and their remaining son, Mary went bravely about the business of living.

Late in 1850 another new baby arrived in the Lincoln household. They named him William Wallace for Mary's brother-in-law who was married to Frances Todd. Soon they began to call the baby Willie, and Willie he stayed.

There was one more son born in the house on Eighth Street. When he came, his mother and father named him Thomas for Mr. Lincoln's father.

One day Mr. Lincoln was bending over the cradle and admiring his newest son. Like all mothers and fathers, the Lincolns always felt their babies were the brightest and the prettiest of the lot.

"Isn't he smart-looking?" Mary asked her husband.

Mr. Lincoln loved to tease her. "I don't know," he drawled. "Don't you think his head is a little large? Looks like a tadpole to me." So Thomas received the lovable name of Tad.

The home on Eighth Street was a happy one in spite of the fact that Mary still had her quick temper. She would always have it, but her husband knew she meant no harm by it. He never answered her sharp words. He knew she would be sorry for them when her flash of anger ended.

Mary had married a poor man, but their house was filled with people and lively talk and laughter. Mr. Lincoln gathered children as wool

gathers lint. Whenever he came into the house with his own little boys at his heels, several of the neighborhood children came along, too.

Mary would have a plate of cookies or pieces of cake ready for them. She remembered all she had learned from Old Chaney. The youngsters liked her good cooking. They liked her bright, cheery welcome even more.

One day she called little Willie to her. "Would you like to have a party?"

Willie gave a happy shout. "Of course I would, Mama!"

"Then let's write the invitations."

She hurried over to her desk. Willie was close behind her. He watched her pen the first invitation. She wrote in a beautiful, flowing hand.

" 'Willie Lincoln will be pleased to see you, Wednesday afternoon at 3 o'clock,' " she read to the little boy.

"How many children may I ask?"

"As many as you want," she promised rashly. Willie took her at her word.

Next day she worked all morning in the kitchen. She made stacks and stacks of golden teacakes. She squeezed dozens of lemons. Then she hurried to lay out Willie's best suit and a party dress for herself. It was almost time for the young guests.

Late that night Mr. Lincoln came home. He had been away all week. He found his boys in bed fast asleep. Mary was stretched out on the sofa.

"What has gone on here?" Mr. Lincoln asked. "The house looks as though the army has just marched through it."

"Worse than that," Mary moaned. "Fifty or sixty little boys. Willie had a party."

"Fifty or sixty little boys!" her husband exclaimed. "Mary, you spoil our sons—and me."

Mary sat up on the sofa. She no longer looked

tired. Her face was one big smile. "But it's such fun, Abraham."

He was now recognized as one of the best lawyers in the West. In 1858 the Illinois Republican Convention made him their candidate for the United States Senate. His opponent was Stephen A. Douglas. Mr. Douglas was a well-known politician and an old friend of Mary's. He was a great orator but small in size. People called Mr. Douglas the Little Giant.

Mary felt that Stephen A. Douglas was not to be compared with her husband. She said, "Mr. Douglas is a very *little* Little Giant by the side of my tall Kentuckian."

Some people felt that slavery was a local problem, which each state had a right to decide for itself. That was what most Southerners said. Mary knew her own brothers said it. Mr. Douglas said it.

Abraham Lincoln said that slavery was not

a local problem, but one for the whole nation to settle.

When Abraham Lincoln was nominated he said, "A house divided against itself cannot stand. I believe our nation cannot endure permanently half slave and half free."

Mary knew he meant that slavery would have to be either everywhere in the country or no-where. The nation must not be broken in two over slavery. The Union must be kept at any cost. That was the all-important thing.

Mary's heart swelled with pride when she heard him speak. She had never forgotten what Grandmother Humphreys had said to her and Betsy so many years ago when they were little girls. Now the time was near when this slavery question would have to be decided once and for all.

"How brave he is!" she thought. "He must win. He cannot lose."

188

Yet he did lose. Douglas became Senator. A disappointed man came home to Mary.

"Never mind," she told him. "You have put up a good fight. You will have another chance."

Another chance came soon. On May 18, 1860, the Chicago Convention of the Republican Party nominated Abraham Lincoln for the Presidency of the United States.

Mary went wild with joy. At last the country was beginning to share the faith she had always held in her tall Kentuckian. She was certain he would be elected.

The weeks that followed were exciting. The Eighth Street house swarmed with newspapermen, cartoonists, and visitors. In the middle of it all Willie came down with scarlet fever.

As election day approached, the noise and hubbub increased. Mary felt that she could hardly wait for the results.

On November 6, which was election day, all

the men and boys in Springfield gathered in front of the telegraph office. Mary was busy at home with Robert, Willie, and Tad. From time to time during the day the latest news was brought to her, but there was no way of telling how the election would end.

Long after midnight Abraham Lincoln hurried home to tell Mary the results. Worn out by the excitement of the past months, she had fallen asleep. He touched her lightly on the shoulder. She awakened instantly. She knew before he spoke.

"Mary! Mary! We are elected!"

Grandmother Humphreys' prophecy had proved right long ago. Mary had married a good man, and he had made her the best of husbands. Now what she had always known in her heart had come true at last. Her Abraham had won the position he deserved—the Presidency of the United States.

He would help the nation through its darkest hour as no one else could. She knew he loved all the people, North and South, white and black.

Soon the Southern states felt they must separate from the North. They formed the Confederate States of America. President Lincoln fought to preserve the Union.

Mary stood beside him in the White House during all the tragic days of the War between the States. She never lost trust in his wisdom and goodness, though her dear and gallant brothers fought and died for the Confederacy in which they believed with all their hearts.